LUCKY DAY

MATT DONNELLY

For L & B,
my Lucky Charms.

The following is based on a true story.
Some of the names and a few locations
have been changed at the request of the Elf B.I.

Also, the ice fishing incident NEVER happened.

1

PROLOGUE

Luck is a mystical phenomenon.

By all measures, from the beginning of time, there have only been two distinct categories of luck: good luck and bad luck. Those blessed with good luck should very well live a life of great fortune. Those cursed with bad luck...well, that's another story.

To the inheritors of misfortune, their existence is filled with challenges. Children with bad luck might have a difficult time learning to ride a bike or solving a math problem or spelling words correctly. They might have trouble squirting ketchup on a hot dog or they might always put the wrong shoe on the right foot.

Adults with bad luck tend to be forgetful and clumsy. They choose the wrong financial investments or change jobs too soon or have a habit of making friends with weirdos. Bad luck follows these individuals around like a stinky diaper, and no one in the history of the universe has ever enjoyed walking around with a load of bad luck in their pants.

However, as eternal as good luck may be, bad luck does not hold the same permanence. A person with bad luck can—and often does—find good luck. It's rare, but it happens. It takes more work and more effort, but bad luck can in fact be changed.

2

MARCH 13, 2014

The zipper of a well-traveled roller suitcase jammed at the corner, and tiny frays of fabric poked out of the zipper teeth. *Just my luck*, Harrison thought, tugging at the tiny metal zipper tag. He tugged and tugged and tugged, but the suitcase just wouldn't open. The tips of his fingers stung, so he decided to take a break.

Harrison sat on the edge of his bed and looked over the neatly folded clothes piled on the duvet. Earlier in the week, Mom took him to Old Navy with Max to pick up some new shirts and pants. Most of Harrison's clothes had gotten too tight or didn't fit. Mom said Harrison was going through a 12-year-old growth spurt. Harrison wished he didn't have to use up a whole day of Spring Break to go shopping with Mom. How embarrassing.

Harrison took the winter coat off the bed and tossed it in the closet. Thinking better of it, and anticipating that Mom would wonder how his coat ended up on the floor, Harrison picked it up and hanged it on a white plastic hanger. It was

March, but the temperature in Silver Spring had warmed to sweatshirt weather.

Harrison opened the weather app on his new iPhone—a gift for his twelfth birthday—and entered "Savannah, Georgia." Harrison had never been to Savannah, but he figured since it was further south than where he lived and therefore closer to the Earth's equator, then it must be warmer. However, according to the weather app, the temperature wasn't much different than it was at home. He wondered if he'd actually need his bathing suit. Grandma seemed to think it would be pool weather.

"Harrison? How's the packing?" It was Mom calling from downstairs. Harrison rubbed the sting out of his fingers and returned to the suitcase. He took a breath and yanked at the zipper. It wouldn't move. He remembered the time that the zipper on his backpack got stuck one day before second grade. Dad told him not to tug so hard, so Harrison held the flap of the backpack with one hand and gently pulled at the zipper and—VRRRP—the backpack zipped closed. He used the same gentle force on his suitcase and finally got it open.

He could hear footsteps coming up the stairs, so he quickly piled the folded clothes into the suitcase. He had been up in his room for a while and wanted something to show for it. He reached for the last pile—some jeans and slacks and a pair of shorts—and lifted it into the suitcase. Hiding underneath was a framed photo of Dad with his arms around Harrison and Max. It was taken during their trip to Disneyland, the last big trip they had with Dad before he passed away.

A wave of sadness rolled through Harrison's body and swirled into the top of his stomach. It had been more than two years since Dad died, but Harrison still occasionally got sad when he thought about him. Mom says that's okay. Even though she and Dale are getting married in three days, she admits she still gets sad about losing her best friend. But she is also excited about sharing the rest of her life with her boys and Dale. They have become quite a family.

Beside the picture frame laid a silver chain with a tarnished gold ring. It was Dad's wedding band. Harrison wanted to pack the photo and the ring so Dad could be part of the wedding ceremony, though he had not told anybody about his plan. He quickly tucked the picture and the ring under the pants in his suitcase.

"Knock, knock."

Harrison didn't have to turn around to know who was standing behind him. It was Dale. Of course it was Dale. Harrison didn't know a single other person on the planet, man or woman, that would say "knock, knock" instead of just knocking on the door like a normal person. In the history of cheesy grown men, Dale was sharp cheddar.

"Hey Dale," Harrison said, turning around.

"All packed?" Dale rubbed his hands together the way a basketball coach does before the start of a big game. He was nervous and excited and anxious and eager all at once.

"Just about," Harrison said before realizing the picture he packed was not entirely covered. He did his best to nonchalantly slide the folded pants over the frame, but Dale had already spotted it.

"Whatcha got there, champ?" Dale smiled, and Harrison was briefly distracted by Dale's heavenly white teeth.

"It's a picture of me and Max and my dad." Harrison held up the photo so Dale could see it better.

Dale took a few steps into the room and sat on the bed. "You guys look really happy there. Disney World, huh?"

"Disney*land*."

Harrison placed the photo in the suitcase between his pants and his shirts. He wanted to make sure there was enough padding so it wouldn't break on the airplane.

Dale breathed deeply in through his nose. "I know we've discussed this at great length, but I just want to reiterate..."

Harrison knew what was coming. Harrison, Max, and Dale had had the "I-don't-wanna-replace-your-dad" speech about a gazillion times already. Harrison didn't mind. He sort of liked hearing it.

"By no means do I wish to replace your father," Dale stated.

No matter how many times Dale had told Harrison this, it always made Harrison feel a little awkward. He wanted so badly to roll his eyes. But he respected Dale, so he just rolled his eyes in his imagination.

"You father will always be your father. He will always, and I mean *always*, be a part of this family. I just wish I was around to meet him."

Harrison always wondered what Dad would have thought of Dale. Dad probably would've thought Dale was kind of weird, too, but he ultimately would have liked him.

Harrison let Dale run out of words, then looked him in the eye. "I know, Dale. You're a great guy. I'm happy for you and my mom. And it'll be cool to have you around all the time now."

Dale smiled big. His teeth shone so bright, Harrison needed to blink.

Harrison and Dale heard a low rumble outside. As it drew nearer, they could both identify it as the sound of a thirty-year-old Toyota Tercel growling down the street. It stopped right outside the house. Harrison and Dale smiled, for they knew exactly who that was.

And that's when Max ran into the room. "Grandma's here!"

"I heard on WTOP there was an accident on the beltway," Grandma announced as she entered the house.

Grandma liked to talk about traffic and weather, but mostly she liked to talk about all of the new electronics and phone apps she had recently discovered. She wore her favorite oversized hooded sweatshirt and had the sleeves pushed up to her elbows. She popped her bluetooth headset out of her ear and stowed it in the neon yellow fanny pack strapped around her waist.

"A milk truck spilled thousands of gallons of milk all over the highway. Lucky for me, I have Waze on my phone. Got me right around it."

"Hello dear mother," Mom said exiting the kitchen.

"Hello dear daughter."

Mom gave Grandma a quick cheek-kiss and raced upstairs. "Just looking for my passport."

"You are aware that we're only flying to Georgia?"

Mom ignored her as she side-stepped around her boys at the top of the stairs.

"Grandma!" Harrison and Max shouted.

"There's my boys." She wrapped her arms around Harrison and Max. Harrison could smell the Coppertone sunscreen Grandma was wearing. No matter the weather, Grandma always wore Coppertone sunscreen. Harrison imagined Grandma had a secret closet filled with boxes of sunscreen.

"Hello Geraldine," Dale said coming down the stairs.

"Dale-y boy. The groom-to-be. How the heck are ya? You got those wedding day jitters yet?"

"Nope. Just the 'don't-want-to-be-late' jitters." Dale chuckled self-consciously. For whatever reason, he always seemed nervous around Grandma. Maybe it was because of the time he was supposed to arrange for Grandma to take care

7

of Harrison and Max while he and Mom went on vacation but totally screwed up and left Harrison and Max on their own for almost a whole week. It was fifteen months ago, but Dale still felt terrible about that.

"Pack light, I always say. If you forget something, find a Marshall's." She turned her attention to Harrison and Max. "You boys pack your swim trunks?"

Harrison and Max nodded eagerly. They had never been swimming in a pool in March, but Grandma called the hotel and found out the pool was heated.

"Well, let's get the show on the road. Stanley had to push his flight 'til tomorrow due to work, but he wouldn't miss it for the world. He's looking forward to it. He always cries at weddings, the old sap."

"Has anyone seen my passport?" Mom called from upstairs. "I always travel with my passport."

"We need passports?" Max worried. "I don't know where my passport is. What's a passport?"

"You don't have a passport, geek." Harrison headed upstairs to collect his suitcase. Max followed behind.

As Harrison entered his room, he could see a black Chevrolet Suburban pull up in front of the house. It stopped and honked twice. It was their ride to the airport. A man wearing a suit got out and opened the rear tailgate. Harrison remembered the last time a car to the airport was waiting outside. That was the craziest week of Harrison's life. This time, they're all traveling together. Everything was going to go as smoothly as possible. Nothing could possibly go wrong.

Or so he thought.

3

GREENSBORO, NC

I n a cluttered shoebox of a bedroom, Caroline Dorsey kneeled on the floor with her body halfway inside the closet. She removed shoes, flip-flops, sandals, cleats, and two pairs of ice skates. She pushed aside leg warmers, tights, a blue leotard, and a sporty black zipper jacket. As the jacket clumped to the edge of the closet, Caroline could read the partial lettering on the back—Greensboro Figure Skating. She paused and tried to remember the last time she wore the jacket. It felt like ages.

For whatever reason, her memory sparked more urgency to find whatever she was looking for. She rummaged harder, shoveling away an array of blue, red, and white ribbons and four figure skating trophies. She advanced deeper into the closet and pushed aside about a dozen Barbies and a jumbo Ziploc bag filled with Barbie clothes and accessories. In the back of the closet lied a long pink box—a Barbie still in its package. It was a gift from her Uncle Dale when she turned nine a few months ago. It was a 1997 vintage Figure Skater Barbie that Dale had purchased on eBay. Little did he know that she had already given up her dream to be an Olympic figure skater about six months ago, right around the time her father moved out. And Barbies? Relics of a childhood long forgotten.

"Are you packed?" Caroline's mom stated, marching into the room. She scooped up tee-shirts and leggings and started folding them like moms do whenever they encounter heaps of their children's clothing. "I'd like to get on the road before noon."

"I can't find my Uggs."

Caroline's mother peered toward the closet with some disappointment. For whatever reason, Caroline always misplaced her Uggs. "I don't think you'll need those for the wedding, Care-Care."

Caroline huffed. She didn't like being called "Care-Care." Not by her mother, anyway. It was a pet name her dad gave her long ago, back when she had a whole family and she was happy and everything was perfect. Her mom only started calling her Care-Care after the separation.

"You have the new strappy sandals for the ceremony, and you can just wear your sneakers in the car."

"I want my Uggs," Caroline stated defiantly. "Dad gave me those. I need to find them." Caroline remembered the day her father took her shopping. She found the exact Uggs she wanted—suede tan slip-on boots with white fur around the top. They were the most comfortable pair of shoes she had ever owned.

"It's not going to be that cold in Savannah. I don't think boots are going to be necessary."

Caroline surrendered to her closet. The boots were not in there. She sat back on her heels and pushed her hair behind her ear. She wasn't wearing earrings, and her mother noticed.

"You should bring the earrings I gave you. For your birthday. The gold ones."

"I'm not really into earrings these days."

"Let's pack them anyway. You never know. They'll look great with your dress."

Caroline rolled her eyes. Her mother always did that—that thing where moms just assume something will happen the way they want it to no matter how firmly their daughters refuse to take part. It's not just the earrings, Caroline thought. It seemed like her mom wanted to control every aspect of her life. Back when Caroline quit skating, her mom freaked out. She threatened to ground Caroline for a week for every practice she missed. In the end, her mom gave in. It was a losing battle. Caroline thought that maybe if she resisted enough, she wouldn't have to go to her Uncle Dale's wedding.

"Can I just go to Dad's this weekend?"

Her mother folded her arms and sat on the bed. Caroline wasn't sure if she was angry or sad or disappointed or what. It didn't matter to Caroline. Not much mattered to Caroline these days.

"Dale is your uncle," her mother said. "You're his only niece. He'd be so sad if you didn't come." She went over to Caroline's dresser and opened the bottom drawer. She pulled out a teal bathing suit and dangled it on one finger. "The hotel has a heated pool. Let's pack your suit."

"I don't wanna go." Caroline held eye contact with her mother for as long as she absolutely could. After what seemed to be a full minute, she blinked away.

"I want you to try to have a good time. Don't ruin Uncle Dale's big weekend. Who knows, maybe you'll end up having fun." Caroline's mother tossed the bathing suit into Caroline's suitcase and started for the door. "And you'll get to meet your new cousins."

Caroline watched her mother leave. She knew there wasn't much use putting up a fight. She was going to Savannah for her uncle's wedding. She didn't have a choice. But in that moment, she didn't like being reminded that she was inheriting two lame boy cousins. She may be forced to meet them, but no one could force her to be nice to them.

4

SAVANNAH

Draped below the Savannah River at the border of Georgia and South Carolina, the city of Savannah is known for its cobblestone streets, historic landmarks, and muggy summer weather. Every year on St. Patrick's Day, thousands and thousands of people descend from all over to take part in the St. Patrick's Day street festivities and experience the long-running St. Patrick's Day parade.

For some reason, Mom and Dale chose to get married on Sunday, March 16—the very day before St. Patrick's Day. Harrison didn't understand why they selected this weekend to get married. They had only been engaged for three months, after all. Had they not booked a block of rooms at the Savannah Country Inn back in January, then it would have been a total disaster.

But Dale insisted on getting married in Savannah. He had fallen in love with the city while studying to become a dentist. If he was ever to get married, he once told his mother, then he would get married in Savannah, Georgia. And if he and his wife ever got lucky enough to have a daughter, then he had a name already picked out, for he loved even saying the name...*Savannah.*

Harrison and Max took their suitcases from the driver and crossed the valet area to the lobby of the hotel. Grandma followed close behind with her bags while Mom and Dale waited for the porter to bring over the luggage cart. Mom had two suitcases, a backpack, and a dress bag. Harrison looked back. They were only staying for four nights, and Mom had a piece of luggage for each night.

Harrison and Max rolled their suitcases into the lobby and plopped down on a stiff couch. It looked fancy, and it looked expensive. But boy did it feel like sitting on a rock.

"We should have two reservations," Grandma told the receptionist.

"Do we get our own room?" Max asked Harrison.

"No. We're staying with Grandma'."

Max grew concerned. "She knows they clean the hotel room before we go in right? She's not going to make us clean it, is she?"

Harrison just shrugged and scanned the lobby. Everything seemed so fancy. There were old paintings in classy frames on the walls, flowers everywhere, and a lot of mirrors. Classical music played softly from somewhere, though Harrison couldn't find any speakers. There were tasteful St. Patrick's Day decorations, and a table that had pamphlets and fliers about events throughout the city for the St. Patrick's Day celebrations. The white inset lights in the ceiling shone brightly off marble floor. And everything smelled like cupcakes and clean laundry.

"So tell me about the pool," Grandma asked the receptionist as they waited for Dale and Mom to arrive. "First and foremost, where is it?" The receptionist handed Grandma a map of the hotel grounds. "Excellente, my dear...Few more questions—Is it open every day?" The receptionist smiled and nodded. "Chlorine or salt water?"

"Chlorine," the receptionist stated, still smiling.

"What's the capacity?"

"I don't know, but it should be posted with the pool rules."

"Rules? Okay. I'll have to review those. May I order food and cocktails out there?"

"Certainly."

"Tell me about the hot tub. Chlorine or salt?"

"Chlorine, like the pool."

By now the receptionist's smile had faded. Grandma was a lot to handle sometimes.

Mom and Dale entered the lobby and approached the reception desk. The porter continued on to the service elevator with the cart full of luggage. Grandma handed Mom a pair of plastic key cards, and Mom turned to address her boys. "Dale and I have a bunch of things we need to take care of, so you'll be with Grandma today."

Harrison and Max simultaneously lifted their hands and gave Mom a thumbs-up.

"Well, what are we waiting for?" Grandma announced. "Get your trunks on, boys, the pool waits for no one!"

5

AS LUCK WOULD HAVE IT

Caroline sat slumped in the back seat of her mother's forest green Ford Fusion, mindlessly playing Angry Birds on her iPod Touch. She had her feet propped on the back of the passenger's seat and kept the door open as her mother packed the car. She could hear her mom rush back into the house and by the sound of her footsteps, Caroline could tell her mom was totally stressing out. It occurred to Caroline that she could offer to help load the car. But it also occurred to her that she was in no way obligated to do anything because she didn't even want to go to the wedding. *Not my problem*, she thought to herself.

She turned off her iPod Touch, already bored of her games, when something outside caught her attention. It was soft-footed but very fast. Was it a deer? A fox? Maybe a stray dog running loose? Whatever it was, it disappeared in the over-grown vacant lot across the street just as Caroline's mom locked up the house.

Caroline could hear her mother's stressed-out footsteps

moving closer to the car. The trunk slammed closed, and her mom loaded into the driver's seat.

"Okay," she said. "I think that's everything." She looked at Caroline in the rearview mirror. Caroline had already started playing another game on her iPod Touch. "Would you like to try to use the restroom one more time? It's a pretty long trip."

"Why couldn't we fly?" Caroline asked, not looking up from her game.

Her mom sighed. They had already discussed this at length. Flying such a short distance was too impractical and too expensive for a single mother.

"It's a one hour plane ride. I looked it up," Caroline said. "It's gonna be like a ten hour drive."

"Oh, it's not that bad. It's only six hours, five if there isn't any traffic. So let's plan for six because you know my luck. We can stop for barbecue when we fill up for gas. Sound good?"

Caroline ignored her. Even though she absolutely loved roadside barbecue, she didn't like agreeing with anything her mother had to say, not since she and her dad separated.

"Be glad you have your little electronic device there," Caroline's mom suggested. "When I was your age, your Uncle Dale and I had to play travel bingo and 'I Spy'. If we were lucky, someone in the car would've thought to bring a 'Where's Waldo' book."

Caroline couldn't believe how lame her mother was. Even as a kid, her mom sounded excruciatingly lame.

"Shoot," her mom said. "I forgot my phone charger. Is it me or have I been more forgetful lately?" She placed a spin of positivity on that statement that bothered Caroline. "Stay put. I'll be back in a flash."

Caroline's mom hopped out of the car and ran into the house. *I'll be back in a flash*, Caroline thought to herself. It sounded like something her Uncle Dale would say. Caroline unlocked her iPod Touch and swiped through four screens of apps. Half of the apps on her iPod hadn't been touched in ages, but for some reason Caroline didn't want to delete them. Maybe it's because they were games she played with her dad. She still sees her dad every other weekend, but he's always too busy now to play videogames with her.

Across the street, an angry rustling of bushes grabbed Caroline's attention. Caroline squinted, but the bushes were a little too far away to see clearly. She imagined a small animal was all tangled up. Maybe it was someone's pet—a puppy that got loose, a cat that had wandered off, or maybe a bunny rabbit had been chased. Poor thing. She looked back at the house, then got out of the car and crossed the street.

As Caroline approached the overgrown vacant lot, her sneakers crunched over small bits of gravel and the rustling in the bushes intensified. Whatever was in there could hear her coming closer and seemed to be trying harder to free itself. She moved around to the side of the bush to get a better look, and the rustling suddenly stopped. Caroline looked left, then right. Did it free itself? Where was it?

She approached the bush and pushed aside a swath of green foliage. And that's when she saw it. Her eyes widened and nearly popped out of her nine-year-old skull. It was not a dog or a cat or a rabbit. Nor was it a fox or a deer. It was something so completely unexpected. There, dangling from a strong branch was a...man.

A tiny little man.

6

THE UGGS DEAL

Caroline could not believe what she was seeing. The tiny little man dangling from a bush branch looked like a grown up, but he was not taller than her suitcase. He had bushy brown hair that touched his bushy brown eyebrows and matched his bushy brown beard. The beard, oddly, had no mustache, and Caroline could see the glistening of sweat on the little man's upper lip. His cheeks were rosy red, and his ears were disproportionately large for the size of his head. He wore dark purple denim overalls and an orange turtleneck. And on his feet, a pair of suede Uggs—Caroline's Uggs!

"Hey," Caroline said forcefully, but the little man did not respond. His eyes were closed, and his arms dangled at his side. But he was breathing. Caroline could hear the whistling of air as he inhaled through his slightly congested nose. Was he asleep? Passed out? Was he playing dead?

Caroline spotted a snapped branch hooking the back of the little man's overalls. The Uggs that belonged to Caroline but were somehow on this man's feet tickled the surface of the ground. He was stuck, and it seemed like he wouldn't be going anywhere without someone's help.

"Hello?" Caroline shook the bush to get the little man's attention. "Can you hear me?"

The man finally opened his eyes and peered at Caroline. He didn't seem happy to see her. He didn't seem relieved. If anything, he seemed annoyed.

"Oh, so you *can* hear me," Caroline said, folding her arms across her chest.

"Yeah, so what?" the little man said. He windmilled his arms, trying to jiggle himself free.

"Those boots you're wearing. They're mine."

"No they are not, you dumb little girl. I found them fair and square."

"You found them? Found them where? In my closet? How did you get in my room, you little thief?"

The little man struggled harder to get free, but it was no use. He was on that branch good. It was not going to bend or snap. Caroline watched as the little man pathetically grappled with nature. She started to feel bad for the little guy. She couldn't take it anymore. "I can help you," she offered.

"I don't need your help, you greasy swine!" The man was very angry. The sweat on his upper lip started to bead like moisture on the side of a soda can.

Caroline didn't appreciate being called names. But the fact remained that this poor little man wasn't going anywhere. "Yes you do," Caroline argued.

"No I don't."

"Yes you do. You're just being stubborn."

"Fine. If you want to help, then don't just stand there like a fire hydrant."

Caroline stared at the little man. She couldn't understand

why someone that desperately needed help would be so rude to his or her only option for assistance. Still, she was willing to help, if nothing more than to get her favorite boots back.

"I'll make you a deal. I'll help you, but I want my Uggs back. They were a gift from my dad and they're the most comfortable shoes I own."

The little man looked down at his feet. "They are extraordinarily comfortable. And they fit my feet just right. But they're mine now!"

"They're no use to you if you're stuck on a branch for the rest of your life." Caroline made a very good point. "I'll help you off the branch if you promise to give me my boots back."

The man clapped the boots together. He started to swing gently until the loop of his overalls slid further down the branch. He took a deep breath and blew it out slowly. He knew he wouldn't be going anywhere without help.

"Fine," he said. "It's a deal. But you need to get me off this stinking branch first!"

"No way. I want my Uggs first."

"How do I know you won't take your boots and leave me here?"

"How do I know you won't run off as soon as I set you free?"

"Why should I trust you? People always lie and take advantage of me. I'm sick of it!"

The man was steaming angry. He swung his arms and punched the air. Caroline thought about how angry she was when she found out her mom and her dad were separating. She remembered sometimes punching the air like the little man was doing.

"Well...why should I trust you?" Caroline leaned back on her heels, tightening her arms around her chest.

The little man stopped flailing his arms and let his body go limp. He was breathing heavy, like he had just finished running a race. Caroline and the man stared at one another. They were at a stalemate.

"Caroline!" her mom called. "C'mon, baby, we gotta go."

Caroline waved to her mom and turned back to the little man. "I need to leave now. I have to go to Savannah, and I'll be gone for a few days. I am the only person in the world that knows you are stuck on this branch. I imagine maybe a fox might pick up the scent, but I doubt a fox would want to help you. It's more likely that it would want to eat you."

"Let me down, and I'll give you your stinking boots!"

Caroline bent over to help the little man. She reached behind him and pushed down the branch, picking up the scent of almond similar to the shampoo her mother uses. "You smell good...for a sweaty little angry man."

SNAP! The branch broke, and the little man tumbled to the ground. He scurried out of the bush.

Caroline walked around to the clearing. "Okay, a deal's a deal. Now hand over my boots."

The little man crouched into a competitive wrestling stance and smiled diabolically at Caroline. "No!"

"What?! We had a deal!"

"I tricked you good, didn't I?!"

"You didn't trick me. You just lied."

The man pointed at Caroline. "You are a baaaaaad luck girl. Bad luck will follow you wherever you go!"

"You're a lying little cheat." Caroline took a step forward. The little man took a step backward. And then something on the ground reflected into Caroline's eyes. She looked down, and there, at her feet, sat a golf ball-sized hunk of gold. It was bright and shiny and polished clean. She crouched down and picked it up. "Bad luck, eh?" she stated matter-of-factly, "Who was the one that got stuck on a bush? And between the two of us, who just found a gold nugget?"

The little man's beady little eyes went wide. "That's mine! That belongs to me! You give that back to me right now, you tyrant!" A look of worry overcame his face as Caroline tightened her grip around the gold.

The little man trembled. "Fine! Whatever you want, take it! Take your boots, just give me the gold."

Caroline felt sorry for the little man. She knew gold was valuable, but for whatever reason, this gold seemed to be the most important thing in the world to him.

"Caroline!" her mom called. "Let's go!"

"Fine. Take off the boots. Slowly." Caroline ordered.

The man slipped off the boots and pinched them at the cuffs. He held them out in surrender. "We exchange at the same time," the man said with a shiver in his voice.

He started toward Caroline, taking small steps, his eyes never leaving Caroline's. Caroline tentatively lifted her hand and opened her palm. The hunk of gold was at the man's eye level. He advanced closer, carefully, his gaze laser focused on the gold. He slipped his free hand under the strap of his overalls when—FLOOP—he disappeared. Boots and all.

Caroline blinked. She blinked again. Was her mind playing tricks on her? She looked all around. She looked in the bush. Where did he go?

"CAROLINE!" her mom shouted.

Caroline took one more look around, then ran across the street.

7

YOU CAN'T CHOOSE YOUR FAMILY

L ocated on the fourth floor terrace of the Savannah Country Inn, the chlorinated pool with an occupancy capacity of one hundred twenty persons overlooked the sprawling Savannah River. A cool breeze wafted up and over the edge of the hotel as the sun descended in the west. While the water temperature was a balmy seventy-two degrees, Harrison and Max preferred the intense heat of the jacuzzi. Grandma had just finished swimming her laps and joined the boys in the hot tub.

"Whoo!" Grandma chirped, slipping into the water. "The hot water's good on the muscles. We need to stay hydrated, though, 'cuz believe it or not we're sweating in here."

Max reached for his complimentary bottle of hotel water and took a sip while Harrison looked around the pool area, observing the empty chaise lounge chairs lining the deck. There were a lot of people staying in the hotel for St. Patrick's Day weekend, but he supposed that for many, March was still too cold to go swimming. That, or everyone else is doing something more fun while he and Max were stewing in a jacuzzi with their grandmother.

"There's nothing to do here," Harrison complained over the noise of the jacuzzi jets.

"Oh, there's plenty to do in Savannah, my dear." Grandma got lost in thought if only for a moment. "It's a beautiful city, and this weekend in particular? It really comes alive. I was here on St. Patrick's Day back in 1999. Your mom was still in college. Your Grandpa and I invited her to join us, but she had other plans for Spring Break. Boy, did we party like it was 1999. I may have been the oldest young woman here, but I'd venture to say I left town with the most beads around my neck. Your grandfather made up this little song for me—'Luck 'O The Irish'—but luck had absolutely nothing to do with that."

Harrison and Max weren't quite sure what she was talking about, but it was clear how fond a memory it was for their grandmother. They also liked hearing stories about their Grandpa. He passed away when they were very young.

"Are we Irish?" Max wondered.

Grandma's eyes darted at Max, as if he had said something to offend her. A silence filled the air. She reached for her bottle of water and slowly removed the cap for a sip. Max looked at Harrison, wanting some reassurance that everything was okay. Was he in trouble or something?

"Young man," Grandma started, pausing dramatically. "Are you meaning to tell me that you are ignorant of your heritage?"

Max just shrugged. He didn't know what "ignorant" or "heritage" meant but assumed it had something to do with being Irish. Grandma looked at Harrison. Harrison shrugged also. "Dad once told us we have ancestors that are from England."

Grandma bowed her head and rubbed her forehead in disappointment. It was as if Harrison just handed her a report card filled with Ds and Fs.

"Yes, that's true," Grandma remarked. "But you also have a good deal of green blood running through those veins of yours."

Green blood? Harrison assumed that meant they *were* Irish. But all of this was news to Harrison and Max. It's not that their mom had intentionally kept this information from them or they didn't care to know. It simply never came up, and they never thought to ask.

"You see," Grandma continued, "my maiden name is Walsh. That was my father's last name. My mother's last name was O'Leary. When I married your grandfather, I took his name—O'Sullivan—which is your mother's maiden name, as you know. Your grandfather's mother's maiden name was Byrne. So, in terms of your mom's side of the family, you pretty much can't get any more Irish than that."

"So...we're English and Irish?" Max wondered.

"Fulwell—the name you inherited from your father—is English as you stated. But we don't hold that against you. You two have the luck of the Irish, like me."

Harrison thought about that for a moment until he was reminded of something. "Dad always said a good man makes his own luck."

Grandma sighed. "That's because he's *English*." Grandma spotted something across the pool and waved. It was Dale, and he was walking with a girl—his niece, Caroline. She wore an oversized black Roblox sweatshirt with the hood pulled over her head.

"Daley-boy!" Grandma called out. Her voice bounced off the stone walls of the terrace.

Dale draped his arm over Caroline's shoulder and guided her over to the jacuzzi. "Hello everyone, I wanted to introduce you to my niece. This is Caroline. Caroline, this is Harrison, Max, and their Grandma Geraldine. Max is nine also."

"Almost ten," Max quickly corrected.

"And Harrison just turned twelve. Maybe the three of you can hang out this weekend." Dale smiled. He enjoyed how families came together at weddings and sincerely hoped Harrison and Max would get along with Caroline. "You know, you three are like cousins now. In fact, after the wedding on Sunday, you *will* be cousins. How about that? Kinda blows your mind, doesn't it?" The question hung in the air with the steam from the hot tub.

"Where are you from, dear?" Grandma asked pleasantly.

"Oh, I'm from Greensboro, ma'am. That's in North Carolina. It's real nice up there."

Grandma smiled, charmed by Caroline's manner and silky Carolina accent. "Well, isn't that wonderful," she said clapping her hands together. "I am delighted to meet you, sweetheart. Why don't you hang out here for a bit while your Uncle Dale and I grab a couple of skinny margaritas. Dale, what do you say? It's my cheat day."

"Oh, I don't know—"

"Nonsense," Grandma interrupted. "I'll get the first round. We can let the kids get acquainted."

Grandma climbed out of the hot tub and pulled on a white bathrobe. She slipped on her banana yellow sandals and escorted Dale out of the pool area. Caroline kicked off her sneakers and sat on a dry spot at the edge of the jacuzzi. She dipped her feet in the hot water.

"Cool sweatshirt," Harrison complimented. He had only

recently started playing Roblox. He was still a "noob," but he wasn't about to admit that to his new cousin.

"Whatever," Caroline remarked. She had never really been good at accepting compliments. Back when she competed in figure skating and placed in the top three in her event, she didn't like dealing with all of the congratulations. But this was much different. The compliment came from a total stranger now purporting to be family. Fat chance, she thought.

"We don't have any cousins," Max stated with a goofy smile. "You're our first."

"So I guess that means your mom and dad are our aunt and uncle now?" Harrison wondered.

"I'm not your stupid cousin."

Max looked at Harrison. Neither of the boys were prepared for such a rude comment to come so swiftly from a brand new family member. "Okay..." Harrison muttered.

"I'll never be your cousin. I don't care who marries who."

"My dad used to say you can choose your friends, but you can't choose your family." Harrison did his best to lighten the mood.

"Your dad died, right?"

Harrison nodded. Max sunk into the hot water, not particularly enjoying the conversation or the way his new cousin made him feel. Caroline stood up and shook the water off her feet before collecting her sneakers.

"My dad's not dead, just divorced."

She turned and headed back into the hotel, never looking back. Harrison thought about some of his friends whose parents got divorced. He knew that sometimes they would feel sad or angry or just sort of be in a bad mood. Harrison wondered if maybe that was the reason Caroline had been so unpleasant to them. At first, he was excited that there'd be another kid to hang out with during the wedding weekend. But after that interaction, Harrison didn't think he'd be spending any time with his new cousin.

But he couldn't be more wrong.

8

THE LUCKIEST BOY IN THE WORLD

The flat screen television mounted above the dark wood chest of drawers was tuned to Food Network. A man with spiky blonde hair and wrap-around sunglasses gorged on barbecue ribs and moaned unintelligible words. The more he ate, the more unintelligible the words, and the more barbecue sauce smeared over his dark blonde goatee.

"Can I change the channel?" Max said from one of the two queen sized beds in the hotel room. He was lying down facing the TV with his chin perched on his hands. Behind him, Harrison rested against a stack of pillows. He had seen "Diners, Drive-Ins, and Dives" before and remembered how hungry the show made him feel.

"Absolutely not," Grandma stated from the other queen sized bed, not taking her eyes off the screen. "Stanley's got me on a Keto diet. This is how I enjoy junk food now."

There was a knock at the door. Max rolled off the bed to answer it.

"How are my loves?!" Mom said, entering. She kissed Max

on the head and strode around the bed and gave Harrison a kiss. And then she started picking up the strewn-about clothes like moms do.

"Fiiiiine," Harrison and Max mumbled.

"Is everyone showered and ready for bed?"

"Yeeeeesssss," the boys droned.

"Hello, dear mother," Mom said to Grandma.

"Hello, dear daughter," Grandma said to Mom.

"I understand you guys met Dale's niece today. She's a little sweetie, isn't she?"

"The sweetest," Grandma said, still watching the spiky-haired man stuffing his face with ribs.

Mom turned toward the boys expectantly. "Well? What'd you boys think of your new cousin?"

Harrison and Max looked at one another, not one hundred percent sure how to answer.

"Boys?" Mom demanded an answer.

Being the bigger brother, Harrison knew he had the responsibility of speaking up first. "She's all right." It was all he could think to say.

"Just all right?" Mom placed her hands on her hips. She sensed the boys weren't telling her something.

"She's kinda mean," Max finally said. "Actually, she was sort of a bully." He felt bad saying that, but he was only being honest.

"I have to say, I'm surprised. She was nothing but pleasant when I met her." Mom took two piles of neatly folded clothes to the chest of drawers.

"Same here," Grandma piped in.

Mom opened Harrison's suitcase and started putting his clothes in the drawers. Harrison thought it was weird to actually put clothes in the hotel drawers. In the past, whenever they stayed in a hotel, they'd always keep their clothes in their suitcases. Or on the floor near their suitcases. But then again, until this trip they had never stayed in a hotel for more than a night or two. Even when they went to Disneyland with Dad, it was only two nights. It's not like they were going to move in.

"She had a long day on the road," Mom reasoned. "She could have been tired, is all. You can spend more time with her tomorrow." Mom lifted a pair of pants out of Harrison's suitcase and spotted the framed photo that Harrison had brought. Beside it, the chain with Dad's wedding ring. "Harrison?" she asked delicately. "What's this?"

Harrison sat up and stiffened, like he'd just been caught sneaking Twinkies out of the snack pantry.

"You brought...Dad's wedding ring?"

"Uh...yeah. I wanted to...well, I thought it would be nice to have Dad here for the wedding...in some way." He dropped his head. He knew he wasn't in trouble, but for some reason it felt like he was. "Is that okay?"

"Oh, baby," Mom pulled Harrison into a tight hug. "Of course it's okay." She wiped a tear from her eye. But it was a happy tear. "What a beautiful gesture. I'm thrilled you thought to include him in all of this. It means so much to me. Thank you, Harrison." She hugged Harrison tighter, and Harrison hugged back. He thought about how sad he was to lose his father. It seemed like ages ago, but it had only been a little more than two years. Back then, he never thought he would be happy again. Now, inside this hotel room with his brother, his mom, and his grandmother, Harrison felt like the luckiest boy in the world.

9

MARCH 14, 2014

The sun had begun to rise over Savannah, and morning dew settled on the bottom half of the windows that lined the hotel corridors. It was quiet in the hotel. The only guests awake were those picking up a newspaper and coffee from the lobby or trotting over to the hotel fitness center. Harrison, Max, and Mom had been up with the sun. Grandma wanted to get a few early morning laps in at the pool, so Mom took the boys down to the lobby for donuts.

A short line had already formed at the cafe. That's okay, Harrison thought. It would give him time to look over the donut options and make a selection. Typically, he would keep it simple and choose something with chocolate icing. Today, he decided he'd keep an open mind because he assumed the donut selection would be as fancy as the hotel.

He wasn't wrong. The donuts encased in glass were shinier and glazier and seemed larger than the donuts they usually got from the Donut King back home. They were as fancy as Harrison expected. His mouth watered. He spotted a particularly appetizing-looking donut. It looked like a chocolate iced donut, but the icing was a lighter brown, more like a tan.

"What's that one?" Harrison asked the barista when it was his turn to order. The barista said it was a maple glazed donut. Harrison had never heard of a maple glazed donut, but it looked too good to pass up. "I'll take that one, please." He smiled politely. It was easy to use good manners when ordering donuts. The barista handed him the donut on a small plate, and Harrison took a bite. It was good. It tasted fancy.

"Do you have any donuts with sprinkles?" Max asked. Max always ordered donuts with sprinkles. Chocolate sprinkles, rainbow sprinkles, he didn't care. If there was a holiday coming up, the Donut King would always set out holiday-themed donuts—red and green sprinkles for Christmas, orange and black sprinkles for Halloween, red and white sprinkles for Valentine's Day.

Harrison looked at the barista apologetically as he took another bite of his fancy-tasting maple-glazed donut. He suspected a lavish hotel like this didn't serve donuts with sprinkles. He hoped the barista would let Max down gently. But then the barista looked into the pastry case. Harrison thought maybe she was doing that to give his brother Max some form of hope. But then, like magic, the barista pulled a small tray of fresh donuts with green sprinkles tastefully scattered over white icing. Harrison couldn't believe it. St. Patrick's Day donuts—of course! Max's eyes grew wide, and his mouth watered.

"Lucky you," the barista said. "These just arrived from the kitchen." She handed Max the warm, glistening, oversized donut on a small plate. Max put his nose close to the donut and could feel the warmth permeating off the sweetened dough.

"Ooh, that looks good," Mom smiled. "I'll take one of those, too."

Harrison eyed the small mountain of fresh St. Patrick's Day-themed donuts, then looked at his half-eaten cold maple glazed donut. Just his luck, he thought.

"Can I have one of those, too?" Harrison asked his mom, who had just taken a huge bite of her donut. With a mouthful of donut, she couldn't speak, and the three little green sprinkles stuck to the corner of her mouth taunted Harrison. He expected his Mom to say no. He expected her to cite the recent rule suggested by the new dentist of the family, Dale. Donuts were a "sometimes food" he'd say. Too many donuts will rot your teeth.

But then, inexplicably, Mom shrugged her shoulders and simply said, "Sure, why not."

Harrison's luck had turned. He knew Mom loved donuts, but this was unexpected. For a long time, Mom was not shy about how much she loved donuts. When she started her Instagram account, there were more photos of colorful donuts than there were of her children. But her love of donuts faded around the time Dad died, and she posted fewer photos.

Harrison remembered a long time ago when Dad gave Mom a special Valentine's Day gift. It was a cardboard cutout of a tree with six colorful round donuts made of laminated construction paper—it was a donut tree. Whenever Mom wanted donuts, she could pick off a donut from her donut tree and give it to Dad, and no matter what Dad was doing, he would drop everything to run to Donut King and pick up a dozen donuts. Every few months, right around Mom's birthday or Mother's Day or Christmas, the tree would magically sprout new donuts, so Mom could have donuts whenever she wanted. Dad couldn't always afford to give Mom a big, expensive present, but there was always love. And donuts.

"I'm stress-eating," Mom stated to no one in particular as they sat at a round wooden table. "Lots to do before the rehearsal dinner tomorrow." She opened up the notes app on her phone and started typing in a few reminders. "Shoot, I haven't confirmed the head count with the caterer." Suddenly, Mom's phone went black. "Oh no!" She pressed and held the phone's power button, but it wouldn't turn on. "I forgot to charge my phone last night. I think it's dead."

Harrison and Max nibbled on their donuts as Mom asked the barista for a pen. She grabbed a few napkins and returned to the table, quickly jotting down a few more thoughts before they escaped her brain.

"Dale's niece and her mom may go bowling later." As stressed as Mom seemed, she still somehow remained calm. "Would you like to join them?"

Harrison and Max looked at each other. After their encounter with Caroline yesterday, the last thing they wanted was to challenge their new cousin-who-didn't-want-to-be-their-cousin to a competitive game of bowling.

"Do we have to?" Harrison said. "I mean, can't we just hang out with Grandma today?"

Mom continued making notes. "Sure, hon. Or you could hang out with George."

The boys' eyebrows nearly jumped off their foreheads.

"George?!"

"Somebody's ears are burning! And it's not from greasy airplane headphones!" shouted an elfish-sized woman crossing the lobby pulling an elfish-sized roller suitcase.

"George!"

10

GEORGE

The little woman stopped and did a little curtsy. "At your service," she grinned.

Harrison and Max smiled wide, and Mom was just as delighted to see her. It was George. George from the North Pole. George who, with the aid of a little sack of X-MA5 a.k.a. Christmas dust, had guided Harrison and Max through the most memorable and infamous week of their short lives.

She pushed down the handle of her suitcase, then ran at the boys and hugged them tight. Harrison and Max had not seen George in more than a year. She had been busy in her new position as Santa Claus's Director of New Media, overseeing a team of fifty app developers, electronics gurus, and general technology nerds, but they stayed in touch as best they could.

"I thought you couldn't make it," Harrison said. He turned to Mom. "Didn't you tell us that George couldn't come to your wedding?"

Mom sheepishly shrugged her shoulders.

"Change of plans," George announced. "New Media

jumped the schedule on account of our new workflow. Padre Christmas decided to hoof it down this way for a last-minute golf trip, so I hitched a ride. Honestly, there isn't much Santa enjoys more than playing a round of golf, and don't ever repeat this, but between you and me, Mrs. Claus has the better short game. There's not a lot of quality golf up at the Pole, as you can imagine. Now, disc golf? There's a sport I can get behind. Most people know it as 'Frisbee golf,' but I'm a purist." George had a funny way of rambling on when she got excited.

"We decided to make it a surprise," Mom admitted.

"Margie in Human Resources said I've got about three weeks' worth of paid time off accrued, and if I don't use it, then I could lose it. So here I am!"

"You get paid?" Harrison wondered.

"Of course I get paid! What—do you think we volunteer up there? Nuh-uh. These sunglasses? Gucci. These shoes? Prada. How else do you think I can afford this swag? Christmas dust?" George laughed to herself. She laughed so hard that Harrison and Max started laughing too, though they weren't quite sure what was so funny.

"So did you bring any? Christmas dust?" Max asked eagerly.

"Not a chance. Not this time around. This visit is strictly of a personal nature. We must make do by our wits alone. That said..." George huddled Harrison and Max closer to her and spoke just above a whisper so Mom couldn't hear. "...I do happen to have brought a certain I-A-T-S-P- J-M."

Harrison and Max had no idea what she was talking about.

"You know, the I-A-T-S-P-J-M..." George winked at the boys. For whatever reason, they still weren't following. Frustrated, George pulled the boys down to her level and whispered, *The Invisible All-Terrain Super Power Jet Mobile?*"

Harrison was shocked. The Invisible All-Terrain Super Power Jet Mobile was something George concocted for Harrison and Max during Naughty Week back in 2012. Harrison assumed the Elf B.I. would have destroyed it by now, or at least locked it away in a secure vault. It broke pretty much every rule of North Pole-sanctioned Christmas gifts.

"You actually got permission to bring the Jet Mobile?" Harrison asked in a whisper.

"Well, I didn't quite get permission," George explained. "But I didn't *not* get permission either, so let's assume everything's on the level. We can take it out for a spin later." George looked around the lobby eagerly, "Now where can an off-duty elf get a slice of breakfast pizza around here?"

11

NEW AUNT JUDY

Harrison and Max returned to their room while George checked in and got settled. Grandma had her robe on and was once again packing a bag for the pool. She had her phone, her Kindle, and her top-of-the-line noise-canceling headphones.

"Do you boys want to join me at the pool?"

"Didn't you just come from the pool?" Max wondered.

"I was doing my laps. Came back for a protein bar and a few things. Now that I got the exercise out of the way, I can relax." She zipped up her bag and flung it over her shoulder. She looked at the boys impatiently. "Well?"

Harrison couldn't imagine going to the pool right now. The day hadn't quite warmed to pool weather. Besides, he and Max were about to venture out with George and check out the city. They only came back to the room for a sweatshirt.

"Suit yourself," Grandma mumbled, popping off a quick text.

Harrison dug into the top drawer and found his sweatshirt neatly folded at the bottom. He yanked it out, and as it dislodged, the chain with Dad's wedding ring flew into the air and bounced under the bed. Harrison quickly scooped it up and placed it safely back in the top drawer. He didn't want that to happen again. It was way too important to lose.

Grandma said her goodbyes and headed out just as Mom arrived with Caroline and her mother.

"Boys, look who I ran into." Mom held the door open so Caroline and her mom could enter. "You've already met Caroline. And this is her mom, Judy, which I believe you'll now be able to call 'Aunt Judy.'"

"Hi Harrison and Max!" their new Aunt Judy beamed. "I've heard so much about you!"

Caroline rolled her eyes, which no one noticed except Harrison.

"What are you guys up to today?" Aunt Judy asked.

"We're about to walk around with George," Max said.

"George?"

"She's a friend from up north, sort of like a big cousin to these guys," Mom explained. "Well, not *big* in the sense that you might think—more like...older cousin. She's actually on the shorter side. Like, real short." It was easier than explaining that somehow Harrison and Max were good friends with a grown-up elf from the North Pole. Trying to explain that was usually followed by *a lot* of questions.

"Oh, 'George,'" Aunt Judy stated, processing. She never considered a woman could be named George. "Is that like 'Georgette?'"

"No, just George." Harrison pulled on his sweatshirt. He could tell his new Aunt Judy seemed perplexed, but it didn't matter to him.

Mom suddenly got an idea. "I know...How about Caroline

joins you? You all can get to know each other and Aunt Judy and I can go get our nails done."

To Harrison and Max, it sounded like the worst plan ever. All they really knew about Caroline was that her parents were divorced and that she seemed like no fun. Caroline wasn't thrilled about the idea, either. But it beat hanging out with her mom all day.

"I think it's a lovely idea," Aunt Judy stated. "Here, take this..." Aunt Judy handed Harrison four twenty dollar bills since he was the oldest. "I was going to take y'all bowling, but go have fun. Treat yourselves to whatever."

Harrison felt the money in his hand. "Eighty dollars?!"

"Sure—go get something to eat, find an arcade or a toy store. Enjoy yourselves."

"That is so generous," Mom said. "Boys, what do you say?"

"Thanks!" the boys exclaimed. Caroline rolled her eyes again, but this time no one noticed.

George suddenly arrived at the door. "All right, all right! Let's go, people! Time is pizza!" She wore a green flowered Aloha shirt, black leggings, and brown cowboy boots. Her Gucci sunglasses were set on top of her head. She took in everyone in the room. "Well, what do we have here?"

"Oh! You must be George!" Aunt Judy was taken aback by how little George was, but she smiled through her surprise as not to seem impolite.

"George, this is Caroline. Is it okay if she joins you guys today?"

"Abso-toot-ly!" George bellowed. "No offense to the smelly boys, but it'll be great to hang with another sister." George slid on her sunglasses. "Now let's get a move on. Pizza don't eat itself!"

12

MR. LUCKY

Harrison, Max, George, and Caroline exited the Savannah Country Inn and started down River Street. It was only just past 11:00 AM, but the kids were ready for lunch and George couldn't wait any longer for pizza. They passed shops, eateries, and little offices in buildings centuries old. On the other side of the street, the Savannah River gleamed in the sun.

Up and down River Street, a certain buzz filled the air. It was Friday, and St. Patrick's Day wasn't until Monday, but it appeared that many grown-ups had not gone to work today. They passed a restaurant that was crowded with college-age students wearing red and white shirts and hats. They were glued to the restaurant's televisions and cheered any time one of the basketball teams scored. Harrison heard a young woman yell, "Go Bulldogs!" A group of men and women in their twenties stood clumped on the sidewalk, laughing and carrying on, and Harrison, Max, George, and Caroline had to step into the bike lane to get around them.

"Is it always this busy here?" Max asked George.

"This is my first time in Savannah," George explained, "but from what I can tell from my peeps on social, it's usually pretty happening, especially here on River Street."

They watched as a young man wearing oversized green sunglasses gave a young woman wearing a green wig a piggy-back ride across the street. Max thought it was funny to watch grown-ups behave like children.

"But this weekend?" George continued. "It's St. Patrick's Day weekend. And St. Patrick's Day isn't until Monday, so these animals have all weekend to party. There's a big parade and a huge street festival tomorrow night. That's one of the reasons I wanted to get down here. Don't get me wrong, I am very excited for your mom and Dale getting hitched, but I've also wanted to do Savannah for St. Patrick's Day for a long time. These are totally my people."

"But the rehearsal dinner is tomorrow," Harrison said.

"And I wouldn't miss it for the world. But I may need to make an Irish exit and sneak out after the speeches." George checked the directions on her phone. She had a list of seven of the best places to get pizza in Savannah, and stop number one was a place called Vinnie Van GoGo's Pizza. They cut over to Bay Street and turned down Barnard Street to Ellis Square. "Then on Sunday," George continued, "I'm all about the wedding. I may need fifteen minutes in the sauna to detox, but I'll be good by the time the ceremony starts."

"Marriage is stupid," Caroline interjected. "And you guys are stupid to think your mom is going to stay married to Dale."

As bright and shiny as it was in Ellis Square, I giant cloud of awkwardness just descended overhead.

"I don't agree with that," Harrison said delicately. He had every right to be offended by what Caroline said, but he also knew that Caroline's parents just went through a divorce. Still, they had only just met Caroline, and she had nothing but nasty things to say.

"Girl, why on earth would you say that?" George countered in a good-natured tone. "Now, okay, I hear ya. Marriage doesn't always work out, sure, and there's statistics to support that, okay, and people change over time, right, but this weekend let's focus on the good and the positive and all the love that's around us, cool?"

Harrison breathed a sigh of relief as the tension mellowed. Caroline nodded, knowing that George was mostly right. Caroline still felt the pain of her parents' divorce, but she didn't know how to articulate it. It was easier to hurt other people's feelings and make them feel the same way she was feeling.

As they approached the edge of Ellis Square, a man in his twenties wobbled in their direction. He wore a giant green sombrero, dark sunglasses, and a green tee shirt that said "Mr. Lucky" across the chest in yellow letters. The shirt was wet around the collar, like he had recently spilled something. Around his neck was a single string of plastic purple beads. He stopped when he spotted George.

"Holy whoa!" he stated in an oozy Georgia drawl. "It's a leprechaun!" His little giggles were followed by snorts of laughter.

George was unamused.

"So, like, I got a question for you, little guy," Mr. Lucky said, though his words weren't easy to understand. Harrison thought that maybe he had just woken up, or that maybe he hadn't actually gone to sleep last night. "So, like, where's your gold? How many wishes do I get?" He snorted louder this time.

George eyed Mr. Lucky, annoyed. "Leprechaun? Are you serious? Do I look like a leprechaun?" She took incredible offense.

45

"Well, yeah, sorta," Mr. Lucky responded.

Harrison eyed George. In her green Aloha shirt, she actually did sort of look like a leprechaun. But Harrison wouldn't have mentioned it, especially now that he knows she didn't like being called that.

"Sir, I am an elf. Elves and leprechauns couldn't be more different. They share no single strand of DNA. It's like we're two completely different species." Harrison, Max, and Caroline listened intently. It was all news to them.

"Leprechauns?" George continued, "They're technically *fairies*. Dirty, smelly fairies with an unhealthy obsession for shiny metal and shoes. The wishes thing? That's not real. But they do have some inter-dimensional powers—*supposedly*—which is why you never see one. Or, if you see one, it's why they suddenly disappear."

Caroline thought about her encounter with the little man yesterday. He was obsessed with her boots and the gold she found. And then he disappeared in the blink of an eye. Could that have been a leprechaun?

George stepped forward and squared up with Mr. Lucky. "We elves have sophistication and class. Leprechauns are begrimed boors! They are the smelliest creatures alive! They smell like trash and moldy deodorant."

George's face turned red with anger. She took a deep breath, collecting herself. She clearly had some prejudices against leprechauns, and Mr. Lucky had set her off.

"Wait...you're an elf?" Mr. Lucky said, confused. "That's Christmas, and this is St. Patty's, right? What day is it? This is, like, tripping me out, man. I gotta go."

George stared at Mr. Lucky as he wobbled away. Her mood had turned sour, but not sour enough to ruin her appetite.

They were only a couple of blocks away from Vinnie Van GoGo's. Pizza would make it all better.

"I met a leprechaun," Caroline said. "He didn't smell that bad."

George eyed Caroline dismissively. "Well, you must not have gotten close enough. You can smell their pungency from fifty meters out. No joke." George slid her sunglasses back over her eyes, snapped her fingers, and pointed in the direction of pizza.

13

CAROLINE'S THING

A piping hot medium cheese pizza slid onto a wooden table in front of Harrison, Max, and Caroline. Another piping hot pizza was placed in front of George. It had so many toppings, you could barely see the cheese. Pepperoni, sausage, ham, bacon, onions, mushrooms, tomatoes, olives. Pretty much everything but green peppers. George liked green peppers, but never on pizza.

Harrison, Max, and Caroline watched as George set a slice on her plate, topped it with grated parmesan and red pepper flakes, and then set a slice on top of that slice, and topped it with grated parmesan and red pepper flakes. She called it a "pizza stack."

"You're gonna eat that whole pizza?" Caroline wondered, eyes agape.

"Eventually," George said, opening her mouth wide and taking a giant bite. Caroline couldn't believe it. Half the double-stacked pizza was gone in an instant. How could such a small person take such a giant bite?

"George loves pizza," Harrison explained. "And the pizza where she's from isn't that great."

"It's *the worst*," George said, chewing her food. 'You people are so lucky, you have no idea. Even gas station pizza here is better than pizza at the Pole."

Caroline rolled her eyes. She didn't want to engage and definitely wasn't going to show interest, though she was somewhat curious about George being an elf. She had never met an elf before and had lots of questions. Nonetheless, she pretended not to care. "Whatever," she dismissed. "Pizza is pizza."

George trained her eyes on Caroline. Obviously, Caroline had never been to the North Pole. Not too many people have, nor would they want to if they knew how bad the pizza was. George wanted to explain, but she let it go. She prepared another pizza stack. "So what's your thing?" she asked Caroline.

Caroline shrugged, nibbling on her slice of plain cheese pizza.

"You gotta have a thing. Everybody has a thing. Flappy here's into Legos and soccer. Harrison just got into Roblox." She took another giant bite of pizza. "So let's have it. What's your deal?"

Caroline stared at her half-eaten slice. The grease on the cheese reflected a neon shamrock that was hanging on the wall. "I don't know, I guess I like video games, but they can be super boring sometimes. I like some of the apps on my phone, but they're getting pretty lame lately."

"So all the stuff you like, you don't like?" George prodded. "Do you play any sports?"

"I used to skate, but it got stupid."

"Skate? Like on a skateboard?" Max asked.

"No, dummy. *Ice skating.* Like, figure skating?"

"We can do without the name-calling, missy." Being the only adult, George felt compelled to say something. There was simply no need for name-calling at this stage in these new cousins' relationship.

Harrison took a tentative bite of his slice of pizza. "Was it too hard? The figure skating?"

Caroline turned defensive. "I was the best on my team. Well, in my age group. But still."

"Then why'd you stop?" Max asked. He knew he wasn't the best player on his soccer team, but it was still fun. And he knew that if he continued to practice, he'd get better.

"I quit after my parents got divorced. The other girls were being jerks, talking about me behind my back and stuff, so I stood up for myself. I got into some fights. Then my coach totally turned on me."

"Did you quit, or were you kicked off the team?" Max asked innocently.

"Does it matter? I'm done with skating."

The truth is, Caroline had a hard time adjusting to separate living situations. It affected her mood and temperament, which is very common. "Anyway, it's not like I was gonna be the next Gracie Gold. I mean, come on."

"I met Gracie Gold when she was at the Olympic trials," George chimed in. "Totally random. I mean *totally.* We share the same birthday." She pulled two more slices of pizza off the tray. "But it sounds to me like you enjoyed skating. Must've been hard to watch the Olympics last month." George suddenly snapped to Harrison and Max, as if she just got reminded of something. "You guys ever been to Sochi? They've got these clubs—'discoteques,' they call 'em—they are...Off. The. Chain."

"You should go back to skating if you miss it," Max urged Caroline.

"I couldn't even if I wanted to. My mom went back to work and I don't have a ride to practice." Caroline took a bite of pizza and looked around the restaurant, trying to take her mind off it. Though she will never admit it, she does miss being on the ice.

Harrison suspected she missed competing. "Do you think if your parents were still together, you'd still be ice skating?"

Caroline just shrugged.

"Chin up, cuz," George stated encouragingly with a mouthful of pizza, "One day, your luck'll change."

"Oh, I'm lucky all right. I've always been lucky. Just yesterday, I found this." Caroline dug into her pocket and removed the golf ball-sized hunk of gold. Harrison and Max's eyes grew wide. George's jaw dropped, and a half-chewed pizza crust dropped out of her mouth.

14

CREAM CHEESE

Harrison, Max, George, and Caroline moved down State Street toward Telfair Square. As they approached the park, the buzzing of the cicadas grew louder. Max couldn't stop thinking about the gold Caroline showed them at Vinnie Van GoGo's Pizza. It was the biggest nugget of gold he had ever seen. Harrison was impressed, too, but he didn't let on.

"Can I see it again? The gold?" Max pleaded.

Caroline felt her pocket to make sure the precious metal was well secured. She suddenly wished she hadn't showed them what she found. "Just forget about it, okay?"

"When you said you met a leprechaun...was that, like, recently?" Harrison started to work out the logic in his brain. He had heard all of the tales about leprechauns and rainbows and pots of gold and all that, but he assumed they were fairy tales. He had certainly never seen a leprechaun in his twelve years of life. But that didn't mean they didn't exist.

"I don't know what it was." Caroline kicked a cracked green plastic cup out of her way. "He was short and sort of angry.

And he was quick. Like, really quick. One minute he was dangling from a branch, and the next minute, he was gone."

George scooped up the green plastic cup and tossed it in a trash can. She then reached into her pocket and produced a small tube of hand sanitizer. She squirted a few drops in her hand and rubbed her palms together. "Trust me, if you encountered a leprechaun, you'd know it. As the sky is blue, you would know it. You would smell like leprechaun for days. I mean, *days*. They claim to live in an entirely different realm or dimension or something along those lines, but they also have a notable reputation for being a bunch of bologna pushers if you know what I mean. So I don't buy the whole parallel universe thing. I believe they live all around us, all over the world."

Harrison, Max, and Caroline listened, captivated, as George sounded off. She seemed to have a lot to say about leprechauns. In fact, she seemed to be an authority on the subject.

"You ever walk by a dumpster and almost barf up your lunch because of the smell? It's probably because there's a whole family of leprechauns living in there." George again reached into her pocket for the tube of hand sanitizer. Just thinking about leprechauns made her want to disinfect. "You ever get the stench of leprechaun on you, there's only one way to get rid of it. And it ain't pleasant. Two words: *Cream cheese*."

Just then, Caroline spotted something across the street. It was a little man sitting at an outside table of an Italian cafe.

And he was wearing...*her Ugg boots!*

15

REVELATION AT AN ITALIAN CAFE

Caroline looked left, then right, checking for oncoming cars. State Street was a one-way road, so cars were only coming from one direction. The light at the intersection of State and Whitaker had not changed, so, without warning, Caroline darted across the empty road.

"*Caroline!*" Harrison hollered after his new cousin, but she had already stepped onto the curb of the opposite sidewalk. Harrison went to follow her, but George grabbed his shirt. At the intersection, the light turned green, and cars charged down State Street. George led Harrison and Max to the crosswalk.

"Hey!" Caroline confronted the little man wearing her Uggs and drinking a chai latte. "Did you follow me to Savannah?"

At first, the little man ignored Caroline. He tried hard to not look at her. But when it became apparent that Caroline wasn't going to leave him alone, he finally acknowledged her. "Why, no," he lied. "I haven't the slightest idea what you are talking about." He sipped his chai latte meaningfully.

"You're wearing my Uggs, you little jerk." Caroline pointed to the little man's feet. From the looks of it, he was indeed wearing her Uggs.

"You must be mistaken," the little man said as politely as he could.

"Those are my Uggs. Size three. My initials are on the inside tag. You were going to give them back to me, but then you disappeared. Where did you go anyway?" Caroline was boiling with anger.

"Once again, you are mistaken," the little man declared. He slipped off one of the boots. "You see, *my* name is on the tag." He held up the boot to show her, and there, written in permanent marker over what looked like the initials "C.D.," which stood for *Caroline Dorsey*, was the name *Padraig*.

"How dumb do you think I am?" Caroline demanded.

Harrison, Max, and George safely crossed the street at the crosswalk. When they arrived at the cafe, they were surprised to see Caroline berating the little man.

"What's going on?" Harrison interrupted.

Caroline stepped back. "This little thief stole my boots."

Padraig blinked nobly and pressed the boot to his chest. "Here I was, trying to enjoy a chai latte on a beautiful spring morn, when this stranger appeared from nowhere and accused me of thievery. I should be offended if I weren't so shocked," Padraig reached for his cup. "I do love chai lattes." But as he reached for his drink, maintaining eye contact with Harrison, he misjudged the distance of his hand to the cup and accidentally tipped it over, spilling the cream-colored chai latte across the small metal table.

Caroline laughed hard, delighted by Padraig's misfortune. She laughed so hard, it made Max uncomfortable. He knew it was mean to laugh at someone's mistake. For a brief moment,

Padraig was overcome by sadness. There was little in life that he enjoyed more than chai lattes. His sadness soon turned to anger.

"Look what you made me do, you little brat!" Padraig spat.

"Okay, hang on now," George interjected. "What exactly is going on here?"

Caroline pointed at Padraig. "He stole my boots back in Greensboro. And now for whatever reason, he followed me and my mom to Savannah."

"That's a lie!" Padraig lied.

The scenario seemed odd to Harrison. If indeed this little man took Caroline's boots, then why would he follow her hundreds of miles to Georgia? "Did you buy those boots, sir?" Harrison asked.

Padraig tightened his grip on the boot. "They are not stolen, if that's what you are implying. I found them! I found them fair and square! And me being in Savannah? Must be a coincidence. I celebrate St. Patrick's Day, too, you know. " He squinted at Caroline. "How do I know you're not following me?! You seem obsessed with Uggs, and I happen to be wearing a pair. Are you trying to steal *my* Uggs?!"

"May I see that boot?" Harrison asked. Padraig relented, handing it over. Harrison inspected it. He looked inside and found the tag. "Padraig?" It was a name he wasn't familiar with.

"That's me," Padraig said emphatically.

"Yeah, your name is definitely written here." Harrison showed Max and George.

"Then if you please, return *my* boot at once."

"But I can also see Caroline's initials. These are Caroline's boots, sir."

"Nonsense!" Padraig erupted.

"We can all see it," George noted. "It's right here, plain as day."

Padraig pressed his lips together, furious. He took three deep breaths. Finally, he pointed a stiff finger at Caroline. "SHE STOLE MY GOLD!"

"I did not steal your gold. You dropped it on the ground, and I picked up, and then you disappeared."

"You tricked me! You tricked me and took my gold!"

Alarmed, George suddenly took a few steps back and covered her nose with her shirt collar as something occurred to Max.

"OHHHHHH!" Max declared. "So you *are* a leprechaun!"

16

PADRAIG

"Everyone back up, I mean it!" George ordered, as if a skunk just scurried onto the sidewalk. Not knowing any better or why, Max backed up and stood behind George. Caroline took a step back as well. Harrison looked at George quizzically. "George, it's okay."

"I'm telling you, the stench of leprechaun can be on you for weeks!" George held a protective arm in front of Max and waved Harrison back.

Padraig folded his arms and stared at George. "You haven't met too many of us leprechauns, have you?"

"I've encountered enough to be traumatized by the stench!"

"How many?" Padraig prodded.

"I don't know, maybe a dozen...and they all STUNK."

Caroline remembered her encounter with the little man in the bush. She advanced forward and sniffed the air. "He doesn't smell bad," she assured.

"Of course I don't smell bad. I bathe regularly, I use shampoo *and* conditioner, and I moisturize." Padraig sniffed the back of his hand and held it up for George to smell. George leaned away.

Harrison introduced himself and the others. Once introductions were made, George cautiously advanced forward. She stopped an arm's length away from Padraig and sniffed a few times. She took a half-step forward and sniffed again.

"I don't get it," she said. She sniffed again. "You look like a leprechaun, you lie like a leprechaun, and you have a leprechaun name...But you don't *smell* like a leprechaun. You don't smell bad at all. In fact," she sniffed again, "you smell pretty darned fantastic. What is that? Herbal Essences?"

"It's an almond-based moisturizer. I use it daily. It's a nice one—I picked it up in New York when I was there last SPD."

"SPD?" Max wondered.

"St. Patrick's Day. They do it pretty big up there."

"I don't believe it," George said. "I thought all leprechauns were smelly, dirty creatures, but you might be the best smelling creature on the planet...Next to Seacrest."

"Seacrest?" Max tried to keep up.

"Ryan Seacreast. I met him in Los Angeles, backstage at a Chris Stapleton concert. Nice guy, Seacrest. Smells fantastic. Heavenly, really. I mean it. Literally. Like, in heaven, I bet people smell like Seacrest. Stapleton? Not so much, but he'd just done two and a half hours on stage."

"I don't care about you and all the friends you have," Padraig interrupted. "I just care about my gold." He reached out his hand toward Caroline and opened his palm. "Give it to me. Please. I really need it back."

"I was going to give it back to you yesterday," Caroline argued. "Can I have my Uggs back now?"

"Yes."

"And you'll actually give them to me this time?"

"Let me apologize...for yesterday." Padraig clasped his hands together. It looked like he was being sincere. "I left...by accident."

"Accident?" Max asked. "Where did you go?"

"It doesn't matter. Now, if you please." Padraig removed the other boot from his foot. Caroline tentatively pulled the gold from her pocket. She still didn't trust Padraig.

"I have an idea," George chimed in. "How about girly over here gives me the gold and smelly over here gives me the Uggs, and on the count of three, we'll swap."

"No! I don't trust you." Pagraig said, cradling the boots. He eyed Harrison. "What about you? You seem like a fair and balanced human."

"Okay." Harrison didn't mind being the broker of the trade.

Padraig held up the Uggs for Harrison to take, but then Caroline reached out to grab them.

"Hey! That wasn't the deal!" Padraig pulled at the boots as Caroline yanked and tugged.

"Caroline? What are you doing?" Harrison held out his hands, hoping to separate them.

"He tricked me once—I'm not gonna let him trick me again." Caroline yanked harder. Padraig tugged back.

"You guys, chill!" George hollered.

The Uggs tug-of-war continued. Caroline yanked, pulling Padraig off balance, when suddenly and inexplicably— FLOOP—they both disappeared.

Harrison, Max, and George stood there, dumbfounded. Caroline and Padraig were gone. In the blink of an eye, they vanished. But where did they go?

Harrison looked around. There was no sign of them anywhere. And then something reflected into his eyes.

There, sitting by his left foot, was Padraig's chunk of gold.

17

ASSESSING THE SITUATION

Harrison and Max searched the patio of the Italian cafe. George came out from inside. Caroline and Padraig weren't in there, either, and no one that worked there had seen anything. Harrison looked up and down the street. Out of ideas, he cupped his hands together and yelled, "CAROLINE!" But she was nowhere to be found.

"Okay, let's assess the situation," George declared. "They were both here, right? And then...they weren't. Do I have that much right?"

Harrison and Max nodded.

"The gold is here, so we know we're not hallucinating."

"Where are the Uggs?" Max wondered.

They looked around, but the boots were gone, too. George scratched her chin. "This is quite perplexing."

"Where could they have gone?!" Harrison worried.

"I don't know! Your guess is as good as mine, bub."

"You know more about leprechauns than we do," Max pointed out.

"I've met a few leprechauns, sure. So what? I'm supposed

to know everything there is to know about leprechauns? I'm an elf. Elves and leprechauns don't really associate, and I think I've been pretty clear as to why, wouldn't you agree? Anyway, if for whatever reason there needs to be some diplomacy between elves and leprechauns, then Ambassador Santa di Clausio usually takes care of it."

"What about the other realm you were talking about?" Harrison wondered.

"Honestly, I'm not a hundred percent sure about that."

"You said there was this whole other universe."

"I said there *might* be. But even if there was, I wouldn't know a thing about how to get there." George started biting her nails, quietly panicking as she realized she was going to be the one deemed responsible for losing a little girl.

"What do we do?" Harrison pleaded. He was worried. They hadn't known their new cousin for more than twenty-four hours, and they had already lost her.

"Maybe we should call the police." Max suggested.

"What good would that do?" Harrison made a good point. If Caroline did in fact disappear into thin air, the police would be of little help.

"I have an idea," George said. "We can go back to the hotel. We can all take naps. And when we wake up, maybe Caroline will be back."

George's idea basically meant waiting and seeing. But Harrison thought the best course of action would be to *actually* take action. "No. We need to do something. We need to find Caroline."

Harrison was right, and George knew it. She racked her brain and chewed her nails. Finally, she had an idea. She wasn't very excited about it, but it was probably the best idea any of them could come up with.

"Santa," she said. "We need to talk to Santa. If there is some sort of leprechaun realm, then Santa would be the one who can sort everything out. I don't like it, I'll probably get sanctioned, but I'm not sure what else we can do."

From the tone of George's voice, Max knew how dire the situation was. However, with the possibility of seeing Santa Claus in the middle of March, Max got a little excited.

"He's not far," George stated. "He's in Augusta. It's about..." She opened her maps app on her phone. "A hundred and thirty miles away."

"That's like a three hour drive!" Harrison worried.

George slipped the phone back in her pocket and slid on her sunglasses. "Not if your driving an Invisible All-Terrain Super Power Jet Mobile."

18

BACK AT THE HOTEL

Harrison, Max, and George entered the hotel and crossed the lobby just as Mom and Dale stepped out of the elevator.

"Hi guys," Mom called out.

"Where's Caroline?" Dale wondered.

"Oh, um, she just had to, uh, run to her room," Harrison lied. He didn't like lying to his mom, but he didn't want her to go into freak-out mode two days before her wedding.

"Is everything okay?" Mom sensed something was up. She always knew when something was up. But she wasn't always distracted with wedding plans.

"Yeah, everything's fine," Harrison said.

"All good, Miss Jenny," George smiled.

"Okay, well, let me know if you need anything. I still have a bunch of things I have to take care of, so if I'm not around, then find your grandmother at the pool."

"We're actually gonna head out again, take in a few more sites." It was sort of a weird thing for a kid to say. Harrison had never been that interested in site-seeing,.

"Okay, well, check in with Grandma later. We're heading out to dinner with some friends that just got into town."

"We should really get going," Dale urged, looking at his watch. "Have fun, you three."

Mom kissed Harrison and Max on the tops of their heads and strode out of the hotel with Dale.

Harrison, Max, and George breathed a collective sigh of relief. But they didn't have much time. They needed to act fast and get to Santa. He was the only one George could think of that could help get Caroline back from wherever she was.

George led the boys out to the parking garage and stopped at the bike rack where a chain bike lock dangled in mid-air. George reached up and pressed something and—THWIP—the Invisible All-Terrain Super Power Jet Mobile appeared.

"Awesome!" Max yelled.

"Cool!" Harrison hollered. It had been a couple Christmases since George made the Jet Mobile for them, and it looked good as new. Harrison remembered George had made two Jet Mobiles that week. She based the design on a Vespa motor scooter but added unauthorized technology like invisibility, gravity seats, and hydro-power so it could run on water. Harrison wondered if the other one still existed and if it was locked away somewhere back at the North Pole.

George stowed the chain in a side compartment and removed two regular-sized helmets and one elf-sized helmet. "Put these on," she said. "The gravity seats oughta keep your fannies locked down, but you can never be too safe." She hopped on and fired up the engine. "Let's ride."

Harrison and Max climbed on as George tapped the invisibility button and—WOOOOOSH—they shot out of the parking garage.

19

SOARING TO AUGUSTA

WOOOOOOSH! The Jet Mobile flew over rooftops and trees at a wind-whipping 140 miles per hour, and Harrison, Max, and George rose higher into the sky. From their vantage point, the expanse was absolutely brilliant. On their left was the state of Georgia, where the Blue Ridge Mountains climbed over the horizon. On their right was the luscious, marshy greens of the South Carolina Lowcountry. Below them, the Savannah River stretched as far as they could see.

"So here's what we're gonna do," George shouted over the wind. "Most likely, we'll have to interrupt Santa on the golf course. He's not going to be thrilled to see me during his golf game, but you let me handle that. We just need him to reach out to his leprechaun contact and explain the situation and that everything's a big misunderstanding. We've got their gold, they've got our Caroline. We make the exchange, bada-bing, everything goes back to normal. I can't imagine the whole shebang will take more than fifteen minutes."

George steered the Jet Mobile down closer to the river, and

their speed created a wake in the slow-moving water. George laughed to herself. "Those leprechauns...they're so funny about their gold, right? I mean, they're obsessed. It's like the elves and that 'Real Housewives' show. You can take away 'Breaking Bad,' but heaven forbid anything happens to 'Real Housewives.'"

George weaved through trees and brought the Jet Mobile back into the sky. "Honestly," she continued, "we'll all probably laugh about this later. Maybe Sanda-Panda will invite some of the leprechauns up for salmon and they'll break bread like dignitaries."

George turned around and looked at Harrison and Max. They still seemed concerned. "Don't worry. We'll have Caroline back by suppertime."

They descended toward Augusta, and George aimed the Jet Mobile toward the lavish green fairways of Augusta National Golf Club, which seemed relatively empty for a beautiful Spring morning.

As they approached the gated entrance, George spotted two groups of men and women in dark suits and sunglasses. It was the Secret Service and—

"Oh no," George gulped. "It's the Elf B.I."

20

DEACON

Harrison, Max, and George quietly waited in a large conference room on one side of a dark brown, oval-shaped table. They sat in high-backed leather chairs that swiveled. Harrison scanned all of the photos on the walls of men holding golf clubs and wearing green blazers as Max swiveled nervously in his chair. George was abnormally quiet. She had a grave look of concern on her face, which Harrison noticed.

"Are you okay?"

George anxiously tapped her finger on the armrest of her chair. "I'm fine. I'm just thinking."

"Is there anything we should be worried about?"

"No, not at all. What's there to be worried about? Who's worried? Why do you ask? Everything's fine."

Harrison sensed George's anxiety. "Are you sure?"

George took a cleansing breath and rubbed her eyes. "It's Deacon," she said.

Harrison tried to remember all of the people from the

North Pole George had mentioned in texts and emails. He couldn't recall anyone named Deacon.

Max stopped spinning. "Who's Deacon?" he asked, a little dizzy.

"He was one of the guys out there with the Secret Service. Deacon is the Deputy Director of the Elf B.I.," George explained. "He rarely travels with the BMOC. He's tough. I don't think he likes me. In fact, I'd venture to say he's not a fan of old George here, not since the ice fishing incident."

Just then, the door to the conference room opened. Harrison, Max, and George sat up straight in their leather swivel chairs. But no one was there. Or, rather, they couldn't see anyone. And that's when Deacon rounded the conference table. He was an intimidating figure in a black suit and tie. A curly-cue wire extended from somewhere under his collar to a small speaker in his right ear. He was large for an elf, about two foot ten, and there was an intensity in his square face behind his dark Oakley sunglasses and special ops beard. Had he been three and a half feet taller, he might've looked like LeBron James. He took off his sunglasses and stared at George, disappointed.

"Deacon! Hey! How are you, big guy?! Long time. What's it been, three months? Company holiday party, right? Good to see you." George tried to keep it light.

Deacon inhaled deeply, then exhaled slowly. "What...are you...doing here?" He spoke methodically and controlled, like he didn't want his words to escape his mouth.

"It's a funny story, really." George's voice shivered. She was tense. Max was anxious, too. Harrison remained focused on the task at hand—to bring Caroline back from wherever she was, regardless of the punishment they were certain to receive.

"You see," George continued, "the boys here and I were

69

with their cousin. We encountered a leprechaun, and—long story short—their cousin disappeared into leprechaun land...we think. We're actually not sure where she went. We're hoping the Big Man might help with that. We've got the leprechaun's gold, so they should be incentivized to make a trade."

"That's not funny," Deacon responded. He wasn't laughing or smiling or looking friendly at all. He leaned forward and sniffed the air. "You said you encountered a leprechaun?"

"Yeah, and that's the thing. This leprechaun, Padraig...he didn't smell bad at all. He actually smelled *good*."

Deacon squinted at George. "You're sure it was a leprechaun?"

"Yeah. He stole Caroline's shoes and everything. But we got his gold. He left it behind when he disappeared with Caroline."

Harrison produced the gold nugget from his pocket, but he could tell Deacon wasn't buying any of their story. Or maybe he always looked that mean. "Sir," he pleaded, "I know this sounds crazy, and we don't mean to disturb Santa Claus, but we don't know what else to do. Caroline—she's my new cousin. Her uncle is marrying my mom in two days. But if we don't get her back tonight, everyone's gonna be worried and it's gonna ruin my mom's weekend and I'd really like to avoid that."

"Wha'dya say, Deac?" George asked in a friendly tone that was probably *too* friendly. Deacon didn't like being called "Deac," especially by George. *Especially* since the ice fishing incident.

"No," Deacon stated.

"I know Santa isn't going to like this," Harrison countered, "but he's our only hope right now."

"No," Deacon said again.

Harrison clasped his hands together. "Please. George said Santa is the only one who can contact someone—a leprechaun ambassador or something."

"You don't understand," Deacon stated. "Mr. Claus is on the seventh hole with President Obama, Phil Mickelson, and Rory McIlroy. Are you actually asking me to interrupt that foursome?"

Harrison, George, and Max stared at Deacon, not sure what to say.

"Also," Deacon continued, "Mr. Claus is currently three under par. He is playing the game of his life."

"It's really important," George implored. "We have no other options."

Deacon took another deep breath and exhaled even slower than the last time. "George," he stated authoritatively, "I know how hard you've been working at the North Pole. You've grown, you're managing New Media now, you've generally been able to stay out of trouble, and I commend you for all of that. Sure, there was the ice fishing thing, but that wasn't all your fault. But right now, you need to make a decision."

Deacon paused dramatically. Harrison, Max, and George sat in their swivel chairs, hanging on every word.

"The way I see it, you have two options," Deacon continued. "I can do what you want and interrupt Mr. Claus during his dream golf game. He won't be happy, but he'll bail you out. Again. It's in his nature. But George—you can expect a lifetime of sanctions. And boys—this all but guarantees a damaging Naughty/Nice report."

Harrison's stomach knotted up. He didn't want to interrupt Santa Claus, but he just didn't know what else to do. Caroline was out there somewhere, and he felt partially responsible for losing her.

71

"Your other option," Deacon suggested, "would be for the three of you to put your minds together and come up with an intelligent solution to work out this problem on your own."

George absorbed Deacon's words, nodding her head, though she didn't quite agree with him. If she thought they could figure this out on their own, then they definitely would've done so back in Savannah. Harrison was thinking the same thing. He wanted to problem-solve, but their problem involved potentially crossing into an alternate dimension, and there was no Youtube video that he could think of to teach him to do that.

"You have the gold, right?" Deacon pointed out. Harrison, Max, and George nodded. "Then that means that smelly leprechaun will be back. Those leprechauns are weird about their gold. I recommend you go back to Savannah, take that gold you have there, and set a trap."

"A leprechaun trap?" Max asked eagerly. He had experience building leprechaun traps.

"Yeah, so, the thing is," George hemmed, "this isn't quite the kind of scenario where we can sit around and wait. Parents are gonna get worried, and if the parents get worried, then the authorities may have to get involved, and if the authorities get involved, well, then Golfy McClaus is gonna hear about it anyway. See what I'm saying?"

Deacon suddenly held up his finger as he heard chirping from the little speaker in his ear. His face turned even more dire. "Mr. Claus just made eagle on the eighth hole. He's beating Phil and Rory, and he's way ahead of the president. I want you to think good and hard. Do you really want me to interrupt the greatest golf game of Mr. Claus's life and make him clean up your mess, or do you want to figure it out on your own?"

By Harrison's estimation, even if they did choose the first option and wanted Deacon to send for Santa Claus, he probably wasn't going to do it. And if getting Santa Claus to help was no longer a viable option, there was only one thing they could do. "You're right, Mr. Deacon," he said, speaking for the group. "We can figure this out on our own." He turned to Max and George. "Right?"

Max smiled. He was with Harrison. He had built a leprechaun trap before, back in first grade, and since then he had ideas on how to improve the design.

"Fine," George agreed. "We'll handle it. But we should get back to Savannah as soon as possible, so I hate to be rude, Deac, but we gotta shove off." George hopped off her chair and headed for the door. The boys followed.

"About that," Deacon stated. "That vehicle you arrived here on? You did not have permission to take it out of the Pole, so we'll be confiscating it."

"The Jet Mobile?! Sure, but I didn't *not* have permission. Come on, can you look the other way this time? I'll totally make it up to you."

Deacon shook his head.

"Is this because of the ice fishing thing? Because that was an accident!"

Deacon just stared at George.

George groaned and complained. "How do you expect us to get back? Can you call in the reindeer for a quick trip south?"

Deacon shook his head again.

"Well, what the heck do you want us to do?"

Deacon shrugged. "Uber?"

21

DRIVER FOUND!

Harrison, Max, and George hustled around Founders Circle of Augusta National Golf Club and down the long driveway toward the main entrance at Washington Road. If they hadn't been in such a hurry, they might have stopped to appreciate the age-old magnolia trees that canopied Magnolia Lane. But they were eager to get back to Savannah. The sooner they got back to Savannah, the sooner they could set their leprechaun trap.

"That Elf B.I. guy Deacon was intense," Harrison noted.

"You have no idea," George said, unlocking her phone. She hurriedly cycled through her apps.

"So what happened during ice fishing?" Max wondered. It seemed like it was a major point of tension between George and Deacon, and Max was very curious.

"Trust me, you don't wanna know." George found the pair of apps she was looking for.

Harrison looked over to see what she was doing. "Are you getting us an Uber?"

"Lately, I prefer Lyft over Uber, but when you're outside of a major metropolitan area, then sometimes you just don't have a choice." She tapped on the Lyft app, but there were no drivers in the area. She opened her Uber app and pressed the "request driver" button. Her phone chimed and a message appeared on the screen—*Driver Found!*—showing exactly one driver about two miles away. "Bingo," she said. "One driver in the whole area, but that's all we need, right? Just one driver to get us back to Savannah." She requested the ride.

"That was fast," Max noted.

"Finally, our luck has changed," Harrison mused. He noticed how the magnolia trees on either side of them arched to make a tunnel that led to the main road, which was lit up by the sun. *There's a light at the end of the tunnel*, he thought.

Then something occurred to Max. "They're gonna drive us all the way to Savannah? That's pretty far, right?"

And then something occurred to Harrison. "Oh yeah. And it's going to be pretty expensive."

"What?!" George blurted, stopping in her tracks. She pushed her phone closer to her face and zoomed in on the driver's picture and name. "Aw jeez! You've gotta be kidding me!"

22
___

SOME KIND OF LUCK

"Jeez Louise!" the Uber driver said to himself as he pulled up to the front gate of the Augusta National Golf Club. "You've gotta be kidding me." It was Jack. Jack Dolan a.k.a Johnny Dolan a.k.a. Little Johnny Dolan a.k.a. The Santa Claws Cat Burglar, but his Uber profile read "Johnathan Dolan."

"Jack?" Harrison asked, squinting at the driver..

"Jack!" Max shouted, recognizing him. It was a total surprise, and even though they shared a somewhat rocky history together, Harrison and Max were glad to see him.

"What are *you* doing here?" George demanded.

"I'm wondering the same thing," Jack stated. These were probably the last three people Jack expected to see in Georgia. It had been fifteen months since the infamous Naughty Week in which Jack double-crossed Harrison and used Max and George to rob the White House. After turning himself in, Jack had spent thirteen of those months in a minimum security prison and was released on excellent behavior.

"I am trying to make a fresh start," admitted Jack. "What's

your excuse?"

"It's kind of a long story." Harrison didn't really want to get into it. They didn't have a lot of time, and they needed to get back to Savannah as soon as possible.

"You know what? Save your breath, I don't want to get involved." Jack seemed bothered. "Given my probation, it's probably not a good idea that I drive you three anywhere. But I can't cancel the ride because I have a spotless Uber record and a five star rating across the board. So if you don't mind, please cancel the ride and let me go about my way."

George looked at her phone. She closed the Uber app and opened the Lyft app. She closed the Lyft app and refreshed the Uber app. "There's no other drivers around," she said dejectedly. "If I cancel this ride, we could be stuck here for hours."

"We don't have that much time," Harrison pleaded with Jack. "We really need to get back to Savannah."

"Savannah?!" Jack wondered. He made a few quick calculations in his head. "That's quite a fare. To be honest, I haven't been able to get a fare since I dropped off that nice Irish golfer. I was hoping to pick up a few rides and work my way back to Atlanta." Jack thought about his situation for a moment, then landed on an idea. "Okay, here's what I'll do...I'll drive the three of you to Savannah, but I expect a reasonable tip and a five star rating."

"Whoa," George countered. "I get you want a tip, and I'm cool with that. But I don't give five stars to just anyone. My drivers need to *earn* their five stars. I don't ask for much—a smooth ride, temperature control, light conversation—but I'm not the kind to promise five stars willy-nilly."

"Fine," Jack conceded, confident he could provide five star service for the duration of the trip. "Let's go."

But then something dawned on George. "Hang on a

second." She held out her arm, keeping Harrison and Max from climbing into Jack's car. "I thought convicted felons couldn't drive Uber."

"Felon?" Jack chuckled nervously. "Felon?! I'll have you know, for the record, there is no one with a record of a felony in this vehicle."

George squinted at Jack. He had to have been lying. He robbed the White House, after all, and he confessed to it. George couldn't understand how Jack wasn't a felon. "How do you figure?" she interrogated.

"Officially," Jack explained, "due to good behavior, impeccable rule-following, and all of the self-help programs I started in the minimum security facility in which I was a guest—"

"Guest?" George cackled. It was no secret he was a *prisoner*.

"—And with a recommendation from Santa Claus and a full presidential pardon, my 'felony' got bumped down to a misdemeanor."

"Barry gave you a pardon?" George couldn't believe it. She thought the president would have been tougher on crime, especially in cases in which his home was invaded.

"Santa said it would look good on his Naughty/Nice report," Jack explained. "Don't act so surprised. I am an upstanding, rehabilitated citizen. Now if we don't get going, then Uber assumes you're a no-show and the ride automatically gets canceled, which...I'd be okay with."

Harrison could tell George was processing everything. The bottom line was that even though Jack went to jail for being the Santa Claws Cat Burglar, he was actually pretty harmless. He was the only ride around. And he was willing to drive them all the way to Savannah and promised five star service. So with that, Harrison, Max, and George climbed into Jack's car and started for Savannah.

23

THE LONG TRIP TO SAVANNAH

Harrison, Max, and George secured themselves in seatbelts in the back seat of Jack's car. Jack checked his mirrors, flicked on his indicator light, and pulled onto Washington Road. As Jack's car motored down the onramp to Georgia State Route 28, Harrison called Mom and explained that they would be back at the hotel around dinnertime. To Harrison, he had not lied. He was optimistic that they would be able to lure Padraig back with the gold and have Caroline returned safely and that everything would be fine.

After Harrison hung up, Max and George breathed a sigh of relief. They knew how good Mom was at identifying a lie, even over a telephone call. George had once joked to Santa Claus that Harrison and Max's mom could consult for the Naughty/Nice Department. She could even *run* it. There was no pulling a fast one on that woman.

"Say, stretch, how long do you think it'll be?" George called from the backseat.

"With traffic, we're looking at three hours." Jack adjusted his smartphone mounted to the dashboard.

George had used rideshare whenever she was in a big metropolis, but this rideshare trip would by far be her longest, most expensive trip yet. "Yikes," she said, realizing what that meant. "This is going to be like a $135 ride."

Jack eyed George in the rearview mirror. "Yeah, well, you could have taken Uber Pool, but that would've added at least an hour."

"Don't worry about the money," Harrison chimed in. "Max and I have some savings and can Venmo you if necessary."

"Nah, don't worry about it," George said. "I'll work some magic with accounting and figure out how to expense this for work so I can turn in my receipt and get reimbursed."

"Are you sure?" Harrison asked.

"Don't sweat it."

Harrison nodded and looked out the window, taking in the lush Georgia countryside. Max put down his window. The air was cool and humid. Trees whipped past as Augusta got smaller behind them.

"Well," Jack said over his shoulder, "it's gonna be a while, so you guys might as well tell me what you're doing in Savannah and how the heck you ended up in Augusta."

"It's kind of a long story," Harrison stated.

"It's kind of a long trip," Jack countered.

Harrison looked at Max and George. They both shrugged —*might as well tell him*. And just as Harrison was about to explain their long journey to Augusta—FLOOP—they disappeared.

24

THE DETOUR

SCREEEEEEEEECH!

Jack slammed on the brakes, and the car spun to a scratching stop on a dirt road. A cloud of brown dust drifted over the hood as Harrison, Max, George, and Jack sat frozen in shock. As the color returned to their faces and the air returned to their lungs, Harrison looked around to make sure everyone was okay.

"What just happened?" Max's voice shuddered with anxiety.

"I...don't know," Jack said, staring straight ahead, still waiting for the dust to settle.

"You run us off the road, stretch? Missed your exit? I'm still dizzy from that blown bootlegger's turn." George rubbed her eyes and unbuckled her seatbelt so she could stand on the seat and get a better look out the window.

"Let's see," Jack analyzed, "We were on the highway...and now, we're clearly no longer on the highway."

"Wow, Jack, your observational skills must be in the ninety-ninth percentile," George uttered sarcastically, "but *how* did we become no longer on the highway?"

Jack tapped on the screen of his smartphone. He had lost his internet connection.

Harrison looked around. Judging by the extreme change in the landscape, it seemed like they were no longer in Georgia.

The four of them took in their surroundings. The dirt road on which the car had stopped was milk chocolate brown. On either side, blankets of lush green grass. Sturdy trees loomed over scattered moss-covered boulders and rocks. There were bushes, shrubs, and plants of varying sizes—a palette of every shade of green imaginable.

"Was there any construction on the road?" Harrison wondered, thinking back to the moments before the spin-out. "Maybe there was construction and the road ended." He had seen that very scenario happen in a movie once.

Jack turned and looked at Harrison square in the eye. "I am a five-star Uber driver. I never take my eyes off the road. If the road ended, I would have seen it."

"I don't know, Jack," George considered, "I feel it would be irresponsible of me to rate this ride so high on the star scale."

Somewhere outside of the car, there was a noise. A faint sound, like someone in the distance was yelling or hollering or calling *Olly olly oxen free!* during a game of Hide & Seek.

"Shh!" Max shushed. "Did you hear that?"

They stopped squabbling and listened. Whatever Max had heard seemed to stop just as everyone quieted down. Isn't that always the case, Harrison wondered.

"Let's take a look around," George suggested, going for the door handle.

They opened the doors and stepped out of the car. The air was crisp and cool, the sun warm on their skin.

"Look at everything," Harrison observed. "It's so...green."

"Greener than green," Max declared. "Even more green than that golf course back in Augusta."

"Don't let Big Red hear you say that, flappy." George hopped onto the roof of the car to get a better vantage point as Max pushed his hair back. He had gotten a haircut last week, but once you get a nickname from George, it's a nickname for life.

George held up her phone as high as she could. "No service," she said dejectedly. "It's like we've teleported back to the Middle Ages.

Harrison looked at his phone. He, too, had no cell phone service. Jack double-checked his phone—not a single bar.

Max walked to the edge of the road, listening intently. He could hear the noise again.

"Heeeeeeeeeeeey!" the voice echoed feebly. Max climbed a boulder and squinted across the bright green horizon. And there in the distance came someone running straight for them.

As it neared them, Max could make out the shape of a girl about his size. "Hey!" he turned to the others, "It's Caroline!"

25

THE MIDDLE OF NOWHERE

Caroline arrived, red faced and out of breath. Even though she had been mean to Harrison and Max at the pool just a day earlier, they were happy to see her. George mentally checked off "Step One" on her imaginary To Do list: *Find the girl.* Jack removed a little bottle of water from a cooler he kept in the trunk of his car and handed it to Caroline.

"Where are we?" Harrison asked.

Caroline thanked Jack for her water and took small sips. Her forehead gleaned with sweat. She was a fast runner. "I'm not sure," she said, catching her breath. "But that lying Padraig still has my Uggs. He took off as soon as we arrived."

"Arrived where?" Jack asked. "What is this?" He was mostly concerned with how far off course they were. Some of the Georgia backroads were treacherous, and Jack was worried about the wear and tear on his car.

"I don't know," Caroline reiterated. And then she squinted at Jack. "Who are you?"

"I'm Jack. Five-star Uber driver."

"Okay?" Caroline didn't see how that was relevant.

"Is this Macon?" George wondered. "Macon, Georgia?" She looked around. "I've never been to Macon, but if you told me this was Macon, then I'd probably be like 'yeah, okay.'"

"As far as I can tell, we're in the middle of nowhere." Caroline hugged herself tightly. Wherever they were, it was as far as she had ever been from home.

Harrison looked over the car for some evidence of what happened, but the car looked as good as it did when it picked them up outside of the Augusta National Golf Club, except for the dust from the road. "Maybe we time-warped or warp-zoned or something," he theorized. As crazy an explanation as it sounded, it was the only explanation anyone offered.

"Well, how do we get back?" Jack worried.

Nobody said anything. Because nobody had any concrete answers. It was as if in the blink of an eye they traveled from one world to another. None of it made any sense.

"The realm," George suggested cryptically. "The leprechaun realm. Maybe this is the realm I've heard about. I didn't buy into it before—it sounded a little too Star Trek-y—but maybe it's true." She scanned the horizon. "I mean, look at all this green...this *does* seem like a place where leprechauns hide out." She sniffed the air. "Oh man, what's that smell? It smells like dirt and foliage. It's so pungent. I knew it!"

"You're just not used to nature because you live in the North Pole," Max explained.

"We got nature up there. Just not like this."

Harrison took in the scene around him. He looked up at the sky. Everything seemed normal, except for the fact that they went from being on a highway to being on a dirt road and nobody could explain how they got there. He couldn't wrap his brain around the possibility of traveling through his reality into an alternate dimension, as George suggested.

Suddenly, there was a crunching of leaves behind a large moss-covered boulder. Caroline whipped around to find the little man wearing her Uggs—*Padraig*. He pointed an angry finger at Harrison: "Give me back my gold!"

26

GREENLAND

Padraig hid sheepishly behind the moss-covered boulder. Outnumbered, he prepared to run if anyone came at him aggressively. But they had the one thing he so desperately needed to get back—the gold. So Padraig tentatively stood his ground.

"Padraig!" Harrison called over. "Where are we?"

Padraig held out his hand like a traffic cop, not wanting them to come any closer. "Stay right where you are and everything will be fine."

"Nobody's moving, stinky," George taunted, even though she knew that in actuality he smelled quite good. She just didn't appreciate how rudely he made his demand. "We kinda just want to know where we are, so we can get a move on."

"You want to know where we are? Look around! What's it look like?" he said sourly.

Harrison, Max, and Caroline again took in their surroundings, but they hadn't been anywhere that looked like this place. Jack had never traveled out of the country. George had traveled to six out of seven continents and considered herself a jet-setter, but she, too, had never visited a place like this.

George eyed the rolling green hills. "So...I guess it looks like...Macon?" she guessed.

Padraig furrowed his thick brow over his eyes. He wasn't sure if George was being serious or if she was goading him. "No!" he spewed angrily. "It's Greenland!"

Harrison scanned the green topography. He remembered his Geography class had briefly covered the country of Greenland, but he didn't remember what it looked like. However, he could point it out on a map, and on the globe in his mind he located it up there in the North Atlantic Ocean between Canada and Iceland. He felt an anxious tingle in his stomach. Had they somehow transported to a completely different country?

"Yeah, okay, I get it," George stated, looking around. "Greenland, sure. Kira and Jax have been to Greenland. This is exactly what they described. I think. They went to Iceland on the same trip. Then Ireland. Anyway, they'd know, and I would totally text them if my phone had any service."

"Wait a minute, hold on, time out!" Jack said nervously. "We're in Greenland? Like, the country?"

Padraig looked confused. "Country?"

"Are you seriously that dumb?" Caroline spat at Padraig. "Greenland is a country, duh." Her cutting remarks seemed to suddenly turn the light and crisp air thick with negative tension.

"THIS IS NO COUNTRY." Padraig climbed down from the boulder and proudly stretched out his arms. "This is our *planet*. Our world. The place of leprechauns and lush plant life as far as the eye can see! *Greenland*. We call it 'Greenland' because it's mostly green. For the same reason you call your planet 'Waterworld.'"

Everyone stared at Padraig, speechless. Did he just call planet Earth...*Waterworld*?

"But we don't call it Waterworld," Max explained. "We call it Earth."

Padraig eyed Max with the stinkiest stink-eye he could contort his face into, then he looked at everyone else. They all seemed to be in agreement with the boy. "But that makes no sense!" Padraig complained. "It's mostly water...like our planet is mostly *green*. 'Earth?' What's the point of calling your planet that? Compared to the water in all of the oceans and lakes and rivers, there's barely any dirt!"

"So let's back it up a minute," George said. "To confirm what each of us are now suspecting, we have somehow crossed into another world or realm or dimension or planet or whatever, and it's called Greenland?"

"Oh my gosh! We warp-zoned?!" Max asked, incredulous.

Padraig nodded matter-of-factly. To him, moving across dimensions was nothing new. He had been tricked into it many times in his life. He didn't think it was a big deal in the way that Harrison, Max, Caroline, George, or Jack would have thought.

"O-kaaaay...so, like, how?" George asked the question that everyone was thinking.

"It was quite simple, actually," Padraig explained, "I set a trap. I wove a net of thin golden fibers and placed it in the road. And then I hid in the gulch and waited. When the tall man's car drove over the net, we were all sent here, to Greenland. Don't you have magic gold back in Waterworld?"

George shook her head. "We've got a little something called X-MA5. Christmas dust, we call it. It's synthetic, unlike gold, very unstable. It's only used for production—meaning no dimensional transfer properties...and it's limited to elves. And if you're wondering—no—I don't have any with me."

"Can you send us back?" Harrison asked. "We need to get back. It's important. My mom is getting married, and if we don't make it back to the hotel soon, then a lot of people are going to worry."

"Yeah, and if I don't get these kids home ASAP," George interjected, "then the resulting hub-bub will end up on my employee record up at the Pole and I'll never be able to leave again, especially after what happened back in 2012."

They were all very concerned and eager to get back to Earth before too long. But of all of them, Jack had the most severe consequence. "If I don't get back by Monday," he announced somberly, "then I can't check in with my parole officer, and they'll send me back to jail. Honestly, I've worked so hard to start a new life. Then the minute I run into these chuckleheads, it's like all of that goes out the window. So whatever we gotta do, we'll do it."

Padraig squinted at the group. "Fine! First...hand over the gold."

"I don't have your stinking gold!" Caroline shouted. "I tried to give it to you outside the cafe and the next thing I knew I was here without the gold and you ran away in my Uggs!"

"I have the gold," Harrison said, digging the gold nugget out of his pocket. He walked over to Padraig and placed the gold in his hand. "There. Now you have it. And if you want to be an honorable man, then you should give those boots back to Caroline. It's only fair. That was the deal."

Padraig pushed the gold into the pocket of his purple overalls and secured it with a little brown button. Then he sat down on a rock and started removing the boots. He hopped off the rock, walked across the dirt in his black stockings, and handed the Uggs to Caroline.

"A deal's a deal," Padraig stated. He looked at Caroline sincerely. "They are very comfortable boots, my darling. Treat them well."

Jack shoved his hands into the air victoriously. "Wonderful! Okay! Cheers to that! Now can we go back to our own planet please?!"

"Yes, can we go back now?" Harrison pleaded.

Padraig shrugged his shoulders. "Well...about that. I don't actually know how to do that. See, I usually get tricked into going to Waterworld, like most leprechauns. The golden net is how I get back, and sometimes I'm not so good at using it." He eyed Caroline, as if to explain how he disappeared so abruptly the day before. "I keep the net with me at all times—it's mandated by the Council and the Chancellor. If they find out I brought you to Greenland, I could get into a lot of trouble. And I'm already not very popular here."

"So how did you figure we would get back?" Harrison asked.

Padraig scratched his chin. "I honestly hadn't that far ahead."

Max's anxiety vibrated through his body. "What are we gonna do?"

"There is one way," Padraig suggested, "but it's much too terrifying. No, I don't think it's an option."

"What is it?" Max asked, his curiosity piqued.

"No. I won't say. Not even as a last resort." Padraig shuddered at the thought.

"If it's a way home, then we would like to know, no matter how scary," Harrison stated.

But Padraig just shook his head.

"Come on, guy, enough with the dramatics," George had tired of the suspense. "What is this terrifyingly terrifying thing that's sooooooo horrible but could also get us home?"

Padraig wrung his hands as he finally swallowed his fear and resolved himself. "It is...a *rainbow*."

27

THE TRUTH ABOUT RAINBOWS

Water and light. That's it. That's all you need to
make a rainbow.

For the people living on Earth, a rainbow is a
phenomenon of weather in which light is refracted, reflected,
and dispersed through water causing a beautiful multi-colored
spectrum of light in the sky. This phenomenon usually occurs
at the exact moment a rainstorm ends and the sun comes out.

At the exact moment when water from the rain meets the
light of the sun.

Most human beings have had the great fortune of experi-
encing a rainbow by their tenth birthdays—unless of course
they live in a place where it never rains. Harrison, Max, and
Caroline happened to live in an area of the world that experienced a good number of rainstorms. In their few years on
Earth, they have each experienced a dozen or so rainbows and
are still fascinated every time a rainbow appears in the sky.

In the North Pole, rainbows aren't as common. But George
has traveled all over the globe and has seen her share of rain-

bows. She even has the instagram posts from Thailand, Australia, and Texas to prove it.

As a seventh grader, Jack entered an experiment entitled "The Magic of Rainbows" into his middle school science fair but was disqualified when the judges discovered he used photos from a National Geographic magazine to pass as his own. It had been a very dry spring, he said in his defense, but his rainbow data was sound. In his research, he had concluded there was absolutely no evidence of magical properties in rainbows.

Just water and light.

Furthermore, there was no evidence to suggest to Jack or anyone that a rainbow could possibly be as terrifying as Padraig made it out to be.

Jack squinted at Padraig skeptically. "What do you mean? About the rainbow? How in the world is a rainbow gonna get us back to Earth?"

Of course, Padraig hadn't considered that. He was only interested in setting his human trap and bringing them to Greenland. Since he didn't know which one of them had his gold, he figured that if he could send everyone into Greenland, then they would have no choice but to hand over the gold. He would be a hero among his peers—the first leprechaun ever to steal *back* gold from humans.

"Well," Padraig explained, "we wait for a rainbow, and then you jump through. That's how it works here. A rainbow appears, and all of us leprechauns lose our minds and run at it. We go crazy. We can't help ourselves. That's why I so deeply dread them. Since we can't stop it, the Chancellor figured out how to use the magical elements of gold to bring us back. Or else we'd be stuck in Waterworld forever."

Harrison looked into the bright blue sky. There wasn't a cloud in sight. "How often do rainbows appear?" he asked.

Padraig's face lit up. "Oh quite frequently. In these parts, we get rainbows every few hours."

The group relaxed a little. That was the best news they could've heard.

But then Padraig scratched his head. "Or is it every few weeks? Yes, that's it—every few weeks.

"Weeks?" Caroline repeated.

"Or is it days? Maybe it's every few days." Padraid folded his arms across his chest and tapped his lips with his finger. "No, it's every few weeks that we see a rainbow. That must be it. I'm not very good with time, actually."

"Every few weeks?" Harrison worried. Mom and Dale's wedding was in two days, but everyone would start worrying if they weren't back at the hotel tonight. They didn't have a few weeks. They didn't have any wiggle room at all.

"What if we needed to speed up that timeline?" George asked Padraig. "What if we needed to get back sooner? Like, much sooner. As in today."

Padraig rubbed his bushy brown beard at the chin. "I suppose there could be a rainbow today, but we just had one yesterday. And two this morning, so..." He looked up at the sky and panned his eyes across the horizon. "Nope. I'm sorry to say, but there likely won't be any rain today."

Max's anxiety was through the roof. "What are we gonna to do?"

Padraig felt badly. He knew most leprechauns in the Township would simply run away after tricking humans. But for some reason, Padraig felt an ache of empathy deep inside his stomach. All his life, Padraig had been very sensitive to others' feelings. He knew he wasn't like the other leprechauns, and the citizens of Greenland reminded him of that every chance they got.

Padraig toed the dirt with his bootless stocking. He wanted to help, but he knew that helping these humans could get him in a lot of trouble. He knew he would be even more ostracized in the Township than he already was. But even though he tried to be like the other leprechauns, his kindness came all too naturally.

"If you don't want to wait for the next rainbow," Padraig explained. "Then I suppose...well, I suppose you could appeal to the Chancellor."

28

THE TOWNSHIP

Padraig led Harrison, Max, Caroline, George, and Jack to the edge of a village. The dirt road curved to one side like a crescent moon, and there were little thatched homes on either side. Smoke billowed peacefully from chimneys as leprechauns bustled about. Some worked in their gardens, some hung wet laundry to dry, and others were simply wandering here and there. Further down the road, there were larger structures, though similarly thatched like the little houses, and even further down the road on top of a hill stood a stone building that looked like a castle.

"Is this where you live?" Max asked, looking around the Township..

"I don't like to give away my personal information to strangers," Padraig said. "This is the way to Castle Greenland." Padraig pointed to the short castle at the far end of the road.

"Do we have to go this way?" George complained. "I'm starting to sense a pungent odor. Is there like a back-way to the castle? A scenic route? Can nobody else smell that?"

All of them sniffed the air. Harrison could smell something

in the air, but it wasn't bad. It was just different. He could smell a wood fire, dry hay, and something cooking like beef stew. "It's not a terrible smell," he stated. "Maybe you're just not used to it. People and places have different smells." Harrison remembered the time he and his family spent a week in Bethany Beach, Delaware. He remembered walking down the boardwalk into town and all of the good smells he encountered— the ocean air, the moist sand, the dry wood of the boardwalk, the savory scent of french fries, the sweet aroma of caramel corn, and sunscreen of course. The sense memory took him right back to that moment, and he suddenly missed his mom and dad.

"I can't take it!" George covered her nose. "It's awful!"

"It's really not that bad," Jack stated, and it seemed everyone else besides George agreed with Jack.

George pushed the collar of her green aloha shirt over her nose. "Who would want to live here?"

"You don't get to choose which part of the world you're born into," Padraig stated.

"Or *which* world you're born into," Harrison noted, taking in this strange yet familiar place.

They started down the road, and as the leprechauns in the village spotted the humans, they dropped everything and ran indoors. It occurred to Harrison that if what Padraig said was true—that humans tricked leprechauns into stealing their gold—then it made sense why these leprechaun villagers would want to hide.

They passed the little homes of the village and entered the Township, where leprechauns busied themselves in markets and shops. But as soon as they saw the human strangers, they ducked behind fruit and produce stands and closed shop doors. Every leprechaun in town hid in fear, except for the ones outside the tavern. They were older men and women by the looks of it, though they weren't much taller than Padraig. They drank mugs of ale and had a lot to say to one another, pointing and yelling and arguing. They stopped when they noticed Padraig with the outsiders.

"Ohhhhhh deary, what have you gotten yourself into this time, butterfingers?" one of them called over.

"Nothing to concern yourself over, Patty," Padraig responded amicably.

"Oy! Do my eyes deceive me or did Padraig find himself a pack of Waterworlders?!" one of the women shouted.

"Maybe they convinced the gullible old fool they were leprechauns!" another woman cackled. She held up her ale as the others laughed with her, and her ale spilled out of her mug and dribbled down her knuckles.

"Never you mind, Patricia," Padraig answered, picking up his pace.

"I'd bet two bits he lost his gold again," shouted a thick-necked leprechaun.

"Lost his boots, too, by the looks of it," a mustachioed leprechaun hollered.

"Well, Pat, that's not all true because I have my gold right here." Padraig held up the nugget of gold he had not but ten minutes ago reclaimed.

"Awwwwww, I reckon the old chum has finally made him some friends! Good for you, chap!" The leprechauns doubled over with laughter.

Harrison looked at Padraig. This time, Padraig did not respond. He was too embarrassed and humiliated and upset to say anything. Harrison felt bad for him. He wanted to say something to the bullying leprechauns, but he didn't want to cause any more problems.

They continued on, leaving the laughing leprechauns behind. Neither Harrison, Max, Caroline, George, or Jack knew what to say. Padraig pretended it didn't bother him, but anyone ganged up on like that would surely have hurt feelings.

Caroline looked back at the leprechauns outside the tavern. There was one thing she wagered they could all agree on. "Those guys stink. They smell like the back alley of a seafood restaurant."

"See?!" George shouted, finally vindicated.

29

THE BOOTS

The dirt road through the Township led to a cobblestone path that stretched up a rolling, grassy hillscape. Beyond the third hill on top of a larger hill stood Castle Greenland. From Harrison's vantage, the castle only seemed to be about the size of a normal two-story house on his block back in Silver Spring. It was made of stone, and Harrison could see columns of moss climbing up its walls.

"Say, Padraig, why do you let those stinkers talk to you like that?" George pulled down her shirt collar, sniffing the air as they started up the first hill.

Padraig didn't want to discuss it.

"I don't know very much about leprechauns," Jack stated. "I mean, I didn't even know there *were* leprechauns until my car ended up here. And I've heard the fairy tales or whatever, but I wouldn't have guessed they'd be such jerks."

"There is nothing I can do about it," Padraig sighed. "Everything they said is true. I am gullible. I am forgetful. I am a klutz. And I get tricked easily. I am sick of being tricked. Of all of the leprechauns in Greenland, I lose the most gold.

Leprechauns aren't supposed to lose gold, so I am an easy target for them. I've lost a lot of gold in my years."

Max took that into consideration. "You've lost the most gold? Like, of all the leprechauns ever?"

"I'm too trusting, I suppose," Padraig answered. "The only way to make friends is to trust. I want to make friends. So I trust people. Just the other day, Patricio asked if he could borrow my boots. I wanted to be friendly, so I gave them to him. But then Patricio never gave them back. When I saw him again outside the tavern, he said he had no recollection of me loaning him his boots, and then the others ganged up on me and told me to stop harassing him."

He paused at the foot of the third hill and looked at Caroline with great sincerity. "Every leprechaun needs a good pair of boots. When I found yours, I thought it would impress the others. And boy did it—until they found out I lost more gold."

Caroline stared at Padraig, softly clapping her Ugg boots together in her hands. She suddenly felt bad for the little guy. He was mean to her, and he called her names, but now...she understood. Suddenly, everything made sense. Yes, he took her favorite boots, and that was the wrong thing to do, but it seemed like he had his good reasons for taking them. He had it pretty hard here in Greenland, and comparatively, she had it pretty good back home. Even though she had a tough, emotional year with her parents' divorcing, she understood she was actually a pretty lucky girl.

She looked around to the others, and then at Padraig. Her eyes landed on his bootless black stockings, now dusty with dirt. She loosened the grip on her Uggs and tossed them over to Padraig.

30

CASTLE GREENLAND

Padraig led everyone into the castle. Inside, their eyes had to adjust. The only light came in through arched holes in the stone walls that served as windows and the few torches that burned orange. Above them, the ceiling was high—for leprechauns—but Jack had to duck ever so slightly to avoid hitting his head. A thin green carpet made a path to a stone table where a leprechaun sat sorting through piles of paperwork. She wore a green knit sweater and glasses above a pointy nose, and she could not be bothered. The thin strip of red hair tucked behind her ear kept dropping over her face. Without looking up from her work, she would tuck it back behind her ear.

A short distance away stood a sign on a wooden stand that read "Wait Here." So they waited. But the the leprechaun receptionist did not acknowledge them. Padraig advanced to the table and rang a gold bell beside a name plate that read "Patricia," and then he moved back to the group.

Harrison squinted at the nameplate. *Patricia.* It seemed like everyone in Greenland was named Pat or Patrick or Patty or Patricia or Padraig. It must get confusing, he thought.

"Um, excuse me?" Padraig said meekly.

Patricia held up one firm finger. She dipped her feathery quill in a hazy inkwell and scratched some notes over the paperwork. She set down the quill and finally raised her eyes to the humans. She didn't seem surprised. Just bothered.

"Greetings, Patricia. My name is Padraig."

"I know who you are," Patricia said sternly. "What have you gotten yourself into this time?"

"Oh, well, I...I am here because, uh, well...it's sort of a long story, but we'd like to speak with the Chancellor."

Patricia looked out the nearest opening in the stone and breathed out dejectedly, as if she had been inconvenienced in the most unimaginable way. She looked over the faces of the group again. It wasn't clear to Harrison if she had ever seen humans before.

Patricia snapped back to work, busily organizing five piles of papers in front of her. "Who are these people?" she asked, still sorting.

"These are some people from Earth," Padraig explained. Patricia eyed him like he had said something in a foreign language. "Er, *Waterworld*," Padraig corrected.

"I can see that," Patricia stated. "What are they doing here?"

Padraig tugged on his overalls. "Well, it's all a bit of a kerfuffle, you see."

Patricia removed her glasses, leaned back in her chair, and folded her arms. She peered down the point of her nose. "This is highly irregular."

Harrison could not agree more. He thought that *everything* about this was irregular. A leprechaun stealing a nine year old girl's boots, the obsession over a small nugget of gold, shifting into an alternate universe—nothing about this could be considered normal in the very least.

"We need to get back," Harrison finally spoke up. "Can the Chancellor help with that?"

Patricia hopped off her chair and moved to a smaller stone table occupied by office supplies. She lifted five clipboards and attached paperwork to each.

"You'll need to fill out these forms," Patricia stated, moving gracefully toward the humans. She handed each a clipboard, which was normal-size for a leprechaun but only about the size of an iPad for humans.

"Do I know you?" George asked. "You ever get to Brazil? Specifically, Rio de Janeiro? More specifically, Carnival?"

Patricia eyed George as she handed each of them small pencils. "Complete each answer," she insisted before returning to the reception table.

Harrison read over the first sheet of paper in the same way he would review a test before answering the questions. The questions were *very* specific:

How often do you lose your socks?

How many lucky shirts do you own?

Do you ever wear lucky underwear? Please explain.

Have you ever broken a window playing ball?

On how many occasions have you broken a window?

What do you do when you find a coin on the ground?

Have you ever wished it would stop raining and shortly thereafter it stopped raining?

How often do you win the lottery?

Is a shooting star just a shooting star? Clarify.

In your opinion, what are the benefits of knocking on wood?

Is it acceptable to spill salt? Why or why not?

Does your favorite sports club win more often than it loses?

Do you prefer even numbers or odd numbers? Explain.

Do you believe everyone in the world is out to get you?

The entire questionnaire was about luck—good luck, bad luck, an individual's opinions about luck. Harrison could tell he was struggling. Max had some serious anxiety when it came to tests, especially if he felt he did not prepare enough.

"Is this really necessary?" Harrison asked, peering out the window. There was still no sign of rain or a rainbow. "We need to get back as soon as possible. My mom is getting married in two days. The rehearsal dinner is tomorrow."

Patricia looked up from her paperwork. "No, this is very important. Answer every question." She returned to her paperwork.

Not wanting to waste time, Harrison and the others thought it best to complete the forms as quickly as possible. It took about twenty-five minutes, and all of them finished at about the same time. They returned the clipboards to Patricia, and Patricia methodically removed the paperwork from each clipboard and returned each clipboard to the supply table.

"Now may they see the Chancellor?" Padraig asked.

Patricia returned to the reception table and sat down, organizing the new forms. "You may not see the Chancellor until you have permission from the Council."

"Then can we see the Council?" Harrison stated with more urgency.

Patricia folded her hands on the desk and eyed Harrison. "The Council is at the tavern for their afternoon libations and won't be back for three hours. You will need to come back then."

31

STRAIGHT TO VOICEMAIL

Back at the Savannah Country Inn, Mom and Dale were in their room getting ready for dinner, none the wiser that Harrison, Max, and the others had plunged into an entirely different dimension. Neither seemed very worried because it was still early afternoon and Mom had received a message from Harrison not too long ago.

Mom reviewed the most recent To Do list on her phone, distracted by all of the things she had yet to accomplish for her big day. But no matter how busy she got, she never forgot that she was a mother. "Any sign of the boys?" she asked Dale. "It's been a few hours since we've heard from them."

Dale picked up his cell phone and dialed Harrison. It went to voicemail. Dale disconnected the call. "They're probably just exploring the city," Dale suggested as he buttoned up a crisp white dress shirt. "Do you want me to try George?"

But Mom was already dialing. By the time she placed the phone to her ear, the call had gone straight to George's voicemail: *It's George, you know what to do!* After the beep, Mom left a message for George asking for Harrison and Max to check in when they got a chance.

"There's a lot to see here," Dale reasoned. "And the cell reception can be spotty. Anyway, they're with George, so I'm sure they're fine."

Mom looked up from her phone and stared at Dale. Dale stared back. "They're with George..." Dale repeated himself, considering what that might mean. "Right. Maybe I'll ask around."

Mom smiled. "Good plan."

Dale slipped on a pair of brown loafers and tucked in his shirt.

32

OUTCAST ON THE OUTSKIRTS

Padraig led the others out of Castle Greenland. He walked everyone over the shallow hillscape, down a long, curvy grass path, and away from the Township. It would be three hours until the Council returned from the tavern, so Padraig thought it best to let his guests rest. He decided he would take them home and make them a meal.

They walked and walked, and Harrison wondered why Padraig's house was so far away from town. They cut down a stone path and then a dirt path and then another path of grass surrounded by trees and headed into a valley where a single thatched house stood a short distance from a pond. A thin wisp of smoke billowed from a tubular chimney, and they could smell the sweet smoke of burning cedar.

As they approached, they got a better view of Padraig's house. While all of the homes and structures in the Township had the same shades of brown and tan, this house had a remarkably unique style. There was color. Lots of it. The front door glowed purple and the shutters on the windows shined bright red. The front side of the house had been painted yellow, while the other three sides were orange. The flat stones that led to the entrance were each a different color, and the surrounding gravel shone blue like the ocean. A rich brown wooden gate surrounded the property.

"Wow," whispered Max. "That's your house?"

Padraig nodded matter-of-factly as he unlatched the wooden gate and welcomed everyone in.

Moments later, they were inside Padraig's home. The decor inside matched the eclectic color-wheel of the exterior. Jack and George reclined in white leather chairs they barely fit into. Harrison, Max, and Caroline sat on a fuzzy crimson couch that was large for leprechauns but small for humans.

Padraig added a few logs to the coals in the fireplace and blew softly onto the embers. He hung a black cauldron above the now-crackling fire and removed a pot of water for tea. He poured six cups of tea and added a small dose of cream and sugar to each. Harrison watched as Padraig worked. For the mean and angry leprechaun he purported to be earlier in the day, he was actually a very decent host.

Caroline sipped her tea. It tasted earthy and sweet and was hot on her tongue but not too hot. She eyed the cauldron over the fire. "What are you cooking?"

Padraig sipped his tea and gulped with satisfaction. "It's a stew."

"I don't eat meat," Caroline declared. She had been a vegetarian for exactly twenty-two days.

Padraig smiled warmly. He seemed much more comfortable in his own home. "Well then you might enjoy this." He nodded toward the cauldron. "It's a vegetable broth with potatoes, carrots, mushrooms, and herbs. A pinch of salt and pepper to bring out the flavors. It's hearty *and* healthy. I hope you like it."

"I'm so hungry I could eat polar bear stew," George announced. "Ever eat polar bear stew, Padraig? Probably not, I'm guessing. It's like elk, only mealier. I don't recommend."

Harrison focused on a silver framed photograph on a navy blue bookshelf. In the picture, a woman is wrapping her arms around what appears to be a younger version of Padraig. "Is that you and your mom?"

"Aye," Padraig affirmed. He looked around the home. "All this color? It's mostly her. She loved color, as did I growing up. Ma used to say that each individual is made up of all the colors of the rainbow. Except that some individuals choose to show only one color at a time. Growing up, I thought about that often. I could choose to show one or two colors like everyone else, but I believe I am destined to show all of my colors." He tugged at the strap of his purple overalls. "Though it makes me something of an outcast."

Padraig moved to the cauldron with six wooden bowls and ladled scoops into each bowl. "I like to cook," he said over his shoulder. "I suppose it's one of my colors."

Bowls were passed around. As they each tasted the stew, smiles formed on their faces. The stew was savory and good. It warmed their bodies but wasn't too heavy on their bellies. It was just right.

"Do you have any neighbors?" Jack wondered. "Or friends nearby?"

"I don't have a lot of friends," Padraig stated, stirring his soup with his spoon. "I don't quite fit in here in Greenland. But I don't want to suppress my colors simply just to fit in. That wouldn't be me, now would it? I have found it's hard making friends."

Everyone agreed. In one form or another, they had all been in Padraig's position at some point in their lives. Whether it was the first day of school, starting a new camp, or meeting people for the first time, making friends had its difficulties. Having friends felt good, but it took hard work. And for all the work that went into making friends and keeping friends, losing friends could happen in an instant. One mean spirited insult or discouraging bit of rudeness could be all that it took to lose a friend. Caroline knew this more than anyone.

Harrison thought about the time he spent a week at basketball camp last summer. He remembered all of the boys there already knew each other. He was the only new kid. He found out quickly that the boys were really into Pokemon. He went home and learned everything he could about Pokemon. The next day, he had something to talk about with the other boys during lunch time.

"Maybe you could find out what the other leprechauns like," Harrison suggested, "and try doing that with them."

Padraig nodded his head knowingly, as if maybe this was something he had already considered. "Leprechauns just want to drink ale and compete in mindless games of chance. They play tricks on humans and other leprechauns during the day, and when they finish with their chores, they go to the tavern and stay there to the wee hours of the morn. The problem is, I don't like the taste of ale, so I don't go to taverns. I like chai lattes. Nobody here likes chai lattes."

"I like chai lattes," George stated in solidarity.

Padraig smiled appreciatively. He imagined George had many friends. She seemed like someone that could make friends in any situation. People are different in that regard. Some people, like George, are quite outgoing. Others, not so much. All Padraig wanted was one friend. One best friend.

Through the window, Padraig spotted a grayness on the horizon. "Oh dear. We should get going."

33

NO SIGN OF THE KIDS

In the lobby restaurant of the Savannah Country Inn, Grandma sat with a man about her age. They were drinking fruity-looking drinks and enjoying being retired. Dale entered the restaurant and scanned the diners.

"Daley boy! Over here!" Grandma called, waving at him. When Dale arrived, she pointed at the man across from her. "You remember Stanley. Stan-baby, say hi to Dale."

Stan stood up and shook Dale's hand. Stan stood about a head taller than Dale. He had broad shoulders and meaty hands. His rosy cheeks stretched with a warm smile. "Good to see you again, Dale. And congratulations on your wedding. Enjoy every minute of it. I've enjoyed four weddings of my own." Stan laughed with Grandma, but Dale was too preoccupied to join in the fun.

"Have you seen the boys, Geraldine?"

And just as Dale asked, Judy entered the restaurant wondering if anyone had seen Caroline. Between the four of them, no one had heard from Harrison, Max, or Caroline in a few hours. They knew they had ventured out with George, who, technically, was an adult. But given the events of December 2012, that certainly could have been cause for some concern.

"Harrison called a little earlier," Dale stated. "it sounded like they were fine and were having a great time. So, I'm sure everything's fine. He said they'd be back by dinnertime, which could mean anything. I bet they'll walk through the lobby any minute now."

They all agreed that if they heard anything or ran into the kids, they would let each other know. None of them was concerned or worried at this point. Simply curious.

34

THE RAINSTORM

Bellies filled with vegetarian potato stew, Harrison, Max, George, Caroline, Jack, and Padraig trekked back to Castle Greenland. As they reached the hillscape that led to the castle, the grayness in the sky darkened, and it started to sprinkle. Then, within seconds, the sprinkling of rain became a great downpour, and the group ran toward the castle.

They pushed open the door, half-drenched, and piled inside. And just as swiftly as the rain arrived, it was gone. Harrison and Max peered out the window. The sun returned. Half the sky was blue and sunny, the other half, dark gray and cloudy. Padraig joined them at the window, and then something suddenly occurred to him.

"Rainbow," he stated urgently. "Look for the rainbow." He hurried from window to window, checking the sky in each direction. "We can get you back to Waterworld if there's a rainbow."

This was great news. Though Harrison didn't understand exactly how a rainbow would get them back to Earth, he understood that rainbows were definitely involved. Everyone scanned the horizon eagerly. They were potentially minutes from being sent home.

Padraig turned to the reception table, but Patricia was not there.

"Oh my gosh!" Harrison blurted. And just as he said it, everyone saw it—the most beautiful, brilliant, bright, vibrant, and vivid rainbow any of them had ever seen in their lives. It stretched across the sky like a bridge in a spectacular arch. The colors were so rich, you could just about reach out and touch them—cherry red, juicy orange, lemon yellow, electric green, deep sea blue, impossible indigo, and velvety violet.

The rainbow reflected in their eyes until a cacophony of laughter snapped them out of it. Their attention turned to the Township in which not dozens, not hundreds, but *thousands* of leprechauns inexplicably ran about like chickens.

"We need to go!" Padraig shouted, his excitement fizzing like a geyser. "NOW!" And in a snap of an instant, Padraig raced out of the castle.

35

THE RAINBOW

H arrison, Max, George, Caroline, and Jack sprinted out of the castle. Padraig had already made it to the bottom of the hillscape and was racing toward the exuberant donnybrook in the Township.

Caroline ran ahead. She was fast. *Really* fast. Harrison and Max tried to keep up, and George and Jack weren't far behind.

"Okay, so there's a rainbow," Jack hollered, panting as he ran. "So what do we do when we get there?"

"Your guess is as good as mine, stretch! " George hollered back.

Harrison looked ahead as he pumped his arms and darted down the final hill of the hillscape. It looked like the rainbow landed just outside the edge of town. Harrison could see a marathon of leprechauns charging toward it.

Ahead, Caroline caught up with Padraig. "Can the rainbow get us back?" she yelled over the din.

"Yes! But we must hurry!" Padraig shouted excitedly, moving as fast as Caroline's Ugg boots could take him.

"What do we do when we get there?"

Padraig smiled wide, overcome with glee as the rainbow reflected in his eyes. "You jump of course!"

Caroline realized she was running ahead of Padraig. She slowed to his pace. "Okay. But where does it take us?!"

"Right where you need to be!"

Padraig sprinted ahead, leaving Caroline behind. Steps away from the base of the rainbow, he jumped and—FLOOP —he disappeared.

Caroline ran after, but the rainbow started to dissipate. The vibrant colors weakened, and the great arch of color faded. As the dark clouds rolled away and the blue sky returned, the rainbow completely disappeared.

And all was quiet in the township.

Caroline slowed to a jog and stopped. Harrison and Max caught up, followed by George and Jack.

"It's gone," Harrison stated, catching his breath.

"And so is Padraig," Caroline noted.

"That was fast," George panted. "It was only here for like thirty seconds."

"I'll say," Max agreed.

George placed her hands on her knees, sucking air. "So that's it? That was our only chance?"

"I thought the little guy was supposed to be helping us," Jack complained.

And that's when Harrison spotted something in the dirt road—a shiny gold nugget—Padraig's gold. Harrison couldn't believe that Padraig had lost his gold yet again. He scooped it up and slid it into his pocket for safe keeping.

"What happens now?" Caroline wondered.

Harrison turned around and looked toward Castle Greenland. "I think we need to go talk to the Council."

36

THE COUNCIL

Harrison led Max, Caroline, George, and Jack into Castle Greenland. Patricia was once again sitting behind the reception table, sorting paperwork and acting as if she had been there all along. But her face was flushed red and her forehead was damp with sweat like she had just been running.

Suddenly twelve leprechauns filed in—men and women, red-faced and sweaty—and marched past everyone. Patricia handed each of them a packet of paperwork as they made their way through a door that read "Council Chambers." Harrison could hear wooden chairs scraping on the other side of the wall, and then it went quiet.

Patricia returned to her seat, folded her fingers together, and then announced, "The Council will see you now."

Harrison, Max, George, Caroline, and Jack entered the Council Chambers. The cavernous room contained one long table that stretched from end to end. All twelve leprechauns of the Council sat on one side of the table, and each of them had a wooden leprechaun-sized gavel. They fidgeted in their seats as they took in the humans. To Harrison, they seemed impatient. To George, they seemed angry and resentful. George once had to appear before a similar council at the North Pole after the infamous missing-Christmas-dust incident. She wasn't particularly partial to councils of any sort.

"By order of the Council," a leprechaun with long auburn hair started, "I hereby declare all five of you GUILTY of the crimes of thievery and malfeasance." She stood up and banged her gavel three times. And then the rest of the leprechauns banged their gavels. The thunderous gaveling echoed off the stone walls. Max pressed his palms to his ears.

Another leprechaun with thick mutton-chop sideburns stood, and the gaveling ceased. And then he announced, "Sentencing shall begin at once!"

He banged his gavel, and the rest of the Council joined him in a cacophonous roar of gaveltry. They pointed and yelled and hollered and accused. Harrison didn't know what to make of it. Were they in trouble? Max and Caroline started to worry. Jack seemed confused. George was unamused.

"Whoa, whoa, whoa!" George shouted. "Guilty of *what*?"

All twelve members of the Council banged their gavels even harder. "ORDAH! ORDAH!" a leprechaun in spectacles shouted.

Harrison stepped forward with his hands open in a show of peace. He and the others had come for the Council's help, but it seemed like they were on trial for some sort of crime. What that crime actually was, no one knew for certain. "I have a question," he stated.

The Council banged and berated until the spectacled leprechaun called for order again. Then he took off his spectacles and pointed them at Harrison. "If the Waterworlder intends to speak, let it be known that everything you say WILL be used against you."

The leprechauns banged and hooted in agreement.

"We were told that you could help us," Harrison said.

The Council banged and banged and banged, much displeased.

"Look," George said, advancing next to Harrison, "we don't want to be here any more than you want us to be here. The thing is, we kinda don't know how to go back to...Waterworld. So anything you could do to help us would be greatly appreciated."

"Who told you we could help you?" the councilwoman with the auburn hair asked.

"Padraig," Caroline responded.

The Council turned unaccountably quiet as they stared at Caroline. Then, all at once, they erupted into laughter, banging their gavels and slapping the table with their free hands.

"What is so darn funny?" George yelled above the din.

"ORDAH! ORDAH!" the leprechaun in spectacles shouted.

The Council settled down, and the leprechaun with mutton-chop sideburns stood to address the humans. "We do not trust Waterworlders on any plane of existence. This is extremely unusual. Waterworlders in Greenland? Extremely unusual. Extremely unusual indeed. And for you Waterworlders to seek advice from Padraig—the absolute worst and unluckiest leprechaun in Greenland—is an ATROCITY."

"Well, we didn't exactly choose—"

BANG BANG BANG BANG BANG, the Council interrupted Harrison with their gavels. "ORDAH!" the spectacled leprechaun yelled.

"You see," Mutton Chops explained, "Padraig comes from a

long line of unlucky leprechauns. It's extremely unusual, I know. An unlucky leprechaun? Extremely unusual. But it's true. Even his grandfather, Paddy, was most unlucky. No family in Greenland has lost more gold than Padraig's. He should be LOCKED UP to avoid the loss of future gold and to protect our home against ANY future invitations of Waterworlders to Greenland!"

The Council banged their gavels in agreement.

"May I say something?" Harrison requested. The Council became unexpectedly silent, allowing it. "I can't speak for Padraig, but maybe if everyone was a little nicer to him and didn't play tricks on him, he wouldn't be so trusting of humans and wouldn't lose so much gold."

"ORDAH!" Spectacles shouted. "May the foreperson read the corresponding statute?"

The long-nosed leprechaun at the end of the row stood and held a piece of paper in her hands. "As be it insofar and unto the decree of henceforth stipulative proceedings and edicts, and to furthermore represent these statutes here forth understood, and by law and rescript of here said requisition and due to the lack of jurisdiction for which Waterworld presides, there is one and only one entity that may and can and should decide the fate of ill-begotten Waterworlders."

The Council surprisingly remained silent as the long-nosed leprechaun returned to her seat. Spectacles sat up to address Harrison and the rest of the humans. There was a graveness on his face. "You must present your case to...the Chancellor."

And with that, the Council stood and quietly filed out of the room, leaving five understandably confused humans in the Council Chambers.

37

THE CLOVER DOOR

A moment passed, and the door of the Council Chambers opened. Patricia entered with an armful of paperwork and scurried to another door. It was a wooden door, large and wide, and it was decorated with carved four-leaf clovers. Without a word to the humans, she slipped a key inside the clover door and unlocked it. She gave the humans a disappointed look, then she stepped through the door. The door creeped closed behind her.

"What's going on?" Max whispered.

Harrison moved for the chamber door that led to the reception area and tried to open it, but it wouldn't budge. George and Jack went to help, but it was no use. Caroline tried the wooden door with the four-leaf clovers, but the door was locked tight.

"They said we need to see the Chancellor," Caroline remembered, pushing on the door. "Do you think the Chancellor is through here?"

Suddenly, there was a clamor from the reception area. The chamber door opened, and a mob of leprechauns—including the Council and the leprechauns from the tavern—pushed Padraig inside. They hurried him to the clover door, and Spectacles unlocked it.

"Hey!" Harrison confronted them. "What's going on?"

Padraig looked at Harrison despondently before being pushed through the door. The leprechauns closed the door, locked it, and headed back through the chamber door to the reception area. As quickly as they arrived, they left.

"Is Padraig in trouble?" Max wondered.

"Flappy, in my experience, it's never a good thing to be forced into a mysterious room by a large mob," George explained.

"Let's get out of here," Jack suggested. He had been standing by the chamber door when the leprechauns left, and he stuck his foot in the door so it wouldn't close all the way. He opened the door wider and checked to see if the coast was clear. "Nobody's out there. Now's our chance."

"I'm with stretch," George agreed. "And you kids are my responsibility. I'd like to avoid you being dragged away by an angry mob."

"We can't leave Padraig," Harrison urged.

"We don't know what's through that door. I think we should go." Caroline walked over and stood beside George and Jack.

Max wasn't sure what to think. On one hand, Padraig was being treated unfairly. But on the other hand, there wasn't much any of them could do about it. Greenland, while a beautiful place, was a strange world with even stranger people. And their rules didn't make any sense.

"Yeah, we could leave Castle Greenland and not look back," Harrison stated. "But then what? What happens when we get out there? We'll be stuck in some alternate universe for the rest of our lives. You heard the Council—the Chancellor is the only one that can help us get back to Earth."

"Unless we wait for a rainbow," Caroline stated.

"But we don't know how long that's gonna take, and if we do get a rainbow, who's to say it'll send us where we need to go?" Harrison eyed the clover door. "I don't know what's through there, but if the Chancellor can help us, then it's worth finding out. And Padraig needs our help. I don't think there's much of a decision to be made here."

Everyone agreed. It would be easy to leave Castle Greenland and run away from the difficult thing, but as Harrison's and Max's dad always said, facing the difficult task head-on means achieving one's goal sooner. There seemed to be only one way home, and that was through the large clover door.

Harrison lightly pressed his hands against one of the carved four-leaf clovers on the door. And then he softly knocked. It was a friendly, undemanding knock.

There was no answer.

Harrison knocked again. This time, more friendly.

Still, no answer.

Finally, Harrison rap-rap-rapped on the door, and on the third rap, the door swung open. It was Patricia.

"The Chancellor will see you now."

38

THE CHANCELLOR

Harrison led the way up the steep stone steps. Max and Caroline followed closely behind with George and Jack bringing up the rear. The stairwell was dark and cool. At the top of the stairs, a single torch burned. They reached the landing and headed down a short corridor that opened into an expansive room. They stopped at the entrance and took in their surroundings.

Light poured in from tall, arched windows, casting a steel gray hue on the stone walls. Between each window hanged gold-framed portraits of Chancellors past—regal-looking leprechauns, male and female. A thin green carpet led the way to five wide stone steps that climbed to an ornate throne with gold flourishes. Sitting on the throne was a short, dignified leprechaun.

"I am Chancellor Patunia," she announced. "Come forward."

Chancellor Patunia was about the size of all of the other leprechauns, but her stateliness made her seem bigger. Small brown freckles dotted her pale face, and creamy strawberry blonde hair curled elegantly over her shoulders. Her sea green eyes kindly reflected the light from the windows. She wore shiny black pants and a white cashmere sweater. Snapped around her shoulders draped a velvet green mantle.

Beside her, Patricia thumbed a stack of paperwork. She selected a document and handed it to the Chancellor.

And at that moment, Harrison noticed something on the right side of the throne. Standing just under the sunlight's reach was a small golden cage—arched at the top like a bird cage. It glowed and shimmered as if an electric current pulsated through. And inside the cage was—

"Padraig," Harrison whispered to the others.

"Okay, this just got weird." George had experienced some weird things in her life, but in her short time in Greenland she had encountered a terrific accumulation of weirdness.

"I'll say," Jack quietly agreed, advancing the group forward. The thin green carpet was smooth and velvety under their feet. Harrison felt the outside of his pocket, making sure Padraig's gold nugget was still there. When they reached the base of the stone steps, they stopped.

Caroline got a better look at Padraig. He looked significantly downtrodden behind the golden bars. "Why is he in there?" she asked sincerely.

Chancellor Patunia furrowed her pale brow as if she didn't understand the question. "Tell me something," the Chancellor stated authoritatively, "if someone in Waterworld squanders the planet's most precious resource, would there be consequences?"

Caroline had to think about that. Earth had many resources, but she wasn't sure which of its resources was most valuable.

"People waste water all the time," George bellowed.

Chancellor Patunia shifted her gaze to George. "And is there any risk of running out of water?"

Max shot up his hand like he wanted to answer a question in school. "No, because it rains, and the planet makes more water."

Chancellor Patunia nodded patiently, prepared to make her point. "And what if your world did not replenish its water? I imagine, over time, the planet would dry up."

None of the humans standing before the Chancellor knew for sure whether that would be true, but it seemed logical. At some point, if there was no more rain or snow and the sun continued to burn as bright, then eventually, perhaps, the water in the oceans and the rivers and the lakes would evaporate and the Earth would indeed dry up.

But then something didn't sit right with George. "I don't get it. We use gold for jewelry and decoration. We use it in some computer electronics up at the Pole, and I think it goes in satellites and cell phones. But it's not like anybody's drinking the stuff like water. You folks need water to survive over here, right? How is gold your most precious resource?"

Chancellor Patunia folded her hands in her lap. "In Greenland, gold contains mystical properties, some of which do not carry over into your world. I know this because I've been there. Here, gold provides heat and light and energy, and it is sustainable, meaning that so long as we have gold, we will always be able to warm our homes and purify our water and keep our fires burning.

She leaned forward and narrowed her eyes. "You Waterworlders...you are takers. Gold is rare in your world, and that makes it valuable. You adore gold because it looks pretty. We require it for survival. Remove our gold—bit by bit—and we will no longer be able to survive. And as much gold as we have in our world now, it is only half of what we had three hundred years ago. Because of you people."

The Chancellor turned to regard Padraig. "No leprechaun in Greenland has squandered more gold in a lifetime than this little leprechaun here."

"If you're sick of humans stealing your gold," Jack argued, "then why not just steal it back?"

"I'm afraid that's impossible. Once the gold exchanges hands from leprechaun to human, it shall remain in your world forever."

"That's not true," Harrison stated. "I have the gold." He dug into his pocket and removed Padraig's gold. "Here. Take it. We don't want it. We never wanted it. We just want to go home."

Chancellor Patunia and Patricia stared at the gold in Harrison's hand. Could this be true? Patricia moved down the stairs and took the gold from Harrison. She climbed the stairs and placed the gold in Chancellor Patunia's hand. The Chancellor turned the gold in her fingers.

"You...brought this from Waterworld?" Chancellor Patunia asked, still dumbfounded.

Harrison nodded as George stepped forward with her finger pointed in the air. "I would like to make sure it goes into the record, uh, if there is a record, that we have gone to great lengths to return that little chunk of gold." She nodded at Chancellor Patunia and stepped back in line with the others.

The Chancellor hovered her free hand over the gold and made a circular motion. The gold nugget glowed in her palm. She reversed direction, and the gold's luminescence dissipated. It looked to Harrison like she was testing its magic powers or something.

"Incredible," the Chancellor stated. She squeezed her hand around the gold. "But it is not enough to simply return what belongs to us," the Chancellor said. "You take and you take and you take. You trick our most gullible, most trusting leprechauns into giving you our gold, and you do it over and over."

"All due respect, Chancellor," Jack chimed in, "but I don't have the slightest idea what you're talking about. I used to steal, but only from other people. Never from leprechauns. Seriously, I didn't know leprechauns existed until a few hours ago. If I knew there was an easy way to get my hands on some gold, then I probably would've taken that route. It seems to me like the five of us are being blamed for the greediness of others, and that's not quite fair, is it? I'd also like to point out again that we did in fact return the gold."

"Returning what is rightfully ours will not be enough," Chancellor Patunia declared. "Would you return egg shells to a hen after you have eaten your spinach and cheese omelette?"

"Uh...no?" George had trouble following the logic.

"What else can we do?" Harrison pleaded. "Name it, we'll do it."

The Chancellor leaned forward in her throne. "As a token of good faith and true contrition, you need to provide our world with more."

"More what?"

"More gold, of course."

"But we don't have any gold," Harrison stated. "What do you expect us to do?"

"That is not my problem." The Chancellor waved her hand, and the cage around Padraig pulsed and throbbed and stretched up and over Caroline.

"Hey!" Caroline shouted.

"Whoa, whoa, whoa—not cool, Chancellor!" George shouted.

"Let her go!" Harrison yelled.

But the Chancellor simply folded her arms and sat back in her throne. "My terms are very clear."

"Excuse me," Caroline pleaded. "I'm the one that got everyone into this mess. I took Padraig's gold. So I should be the one to fix it."

"If you took Padraig's gold, then why did this boy return it?" Chancellor Patunia motioned to Harrison.

"Nobody stole anything," Padraig admitted. "It's my fault, like it always is. I dropped it. I left it behind. Caroline and Harrison just picked it up."

"Very well," Chancellor Patunia stated. She motioned her hand toward the golden cage, and it suddenly throbbed and lifted over Caroline, freeing her. But then the cage bent and twisted and enclosed around Max, George, and Jack.

"Hey!" Harrison yelled, reaching for his brother.

"Aw, Jeez Louise!" Jack complained, tugging at the iridescent-gold bars of the cage.

The Chancellor leaned toward Harrison and Caroline. "You have twenty-four hours. Return to Waterworld and bring me gold of equal or greater value than the gold you stole."

"We didn't steal—"

"If you fail," the Chancellor interrupted. "Then your friends shall forever remain my prisoners."

She waved her hand again, and the golden cage raised over Padraig, freeing him. "Padraig will be your guide. If Padraig fails, then he shall be banished from Greenland and sent to live among the trash and refuse in Waterworld."

"I knew it," George said under her breath.

"Twenty-four hours," Chancellor Patunia repeated.

Harrison looked at Caroline, then at Padraig. Their

problem still remained unsolved. They had no choice but to do what was asked, but how were they to get back to Earth?

Padraig raised his hand to get the Chancellor's attention. "Chancellor, I only know how to get *back* from Waterworld." He removed the golden net from his jacket. "I use this net, and I keep it with me at all times, which is the rule. But without a rainbow, how do we *get* to Waterworld? Is there some magic involved? Or a special password or cape or something?"

"Oh for the love of St. Patrick," Chancellor Patunia stated, waving her hand in their direction and—FLOOP—they disappeared.

39

WAFFLE HOUSE

I n an unassuming breakfast establishment, a large booth sat empty. A server named Stella had just wiped down the table and added six sets of clean silverware and napkins. She moved to the hostess station when—FLOOP—Harrison, Caroline, and Padraig suddenly appeared in the booth.

Harrison caught his bearings and looked around the diner. It was crowded with festive groups of people wearing green and white, and it smelled like bacon, eggs, and coffee. "Are we at a—?"

"Waffle House," Caroline confirmed. She and her mom had been to Waffle House at least once a week since the separation.

"Are we anywhere near the hotel?" Harrison wondered. He looked out the window. Nothing looked familiar.

Caroline scanned the restaurant for clues. "We could be anywhere."

"What terrible luck," Padraig groused. He hung his head low. He couldn't look at Harrison or Caroline in the eye. "We must be the most unlucky, non-luck-having, luck-lacking unlukies in the whole entire universe."

Harrison turned around in his seat. "Excuse me, sir. Where are we?"

The man in the next booth over turned around, surprised at the question. But he smiled neighborly. He had a great smile. Great teeth, too. And he had great hair. And he smelled so, so good. He looked like he was around Harrison's mom's age, and he was having an early breakfast-based supper with an older woman that looked like she was his mom.

"We're at Waffle House," the man said kindly.

"No, I mean, what city are we in?"

The man looked at his mom, who seemed as confused as he was. "We're in Savannah."

Harrison's eyes grew wide and his cheeks broadened into a smile.

"Oh thank goodness," Caroline sighed. She then turned to Padraig. "Looks like our luck just changed."

"You are the lucky ones," Padraig argued. "It follows you around. But if you're born unlucky, like I was, you'll stay unlucky. Sure, occasionally your fortune might turn every now and again, but when all is said and done, the unlucky *stay* unlucky."

From the next booth, the man had overheard the conversation. He seemed bothered by what they were discussing. Finally, he turned around. "What's all this talk about luck?"

Harrison turned to regard the man. "Our friend here has a theory about luck. People born lucky will always be lucky, and people who are born unlucky will always be unlucky."

"Not always," Padraig corrected, "but most of the time."

"You know what I think?" the man asked. But he didn't intend to wait for an answer. "I think there's no such thing as

134

luck. I think people say they're either lucky or unlucky to explain away their insecurities. Or their laziness. People say *I'm* lucky. You know what I tell them? I tell them I work very, very hard. I work all the time. I do pretty well for myself, but it has nothing to do with luck. It's because I'm dedicated."

"My dad said that with hard work and dedication, people make their own luck," Harrison offered.

The man lifted his eyebrows and looked at his mom. "I don't believe in luck. I believe in fortune. I make my *own* fortune. And I have quite a fortune. Let me just say this...if you have a goal, and you really want to achieve that goal, then you need to outwork everyone else that's going after the same goal. But don't think of it as a competition thing. You're only in competition with yourself. So you have to ask yourself: Are you going to achieve that goal or not? Whether you achieve it has absolutely nothing to do with luck. It's about hard work, dedication, and persistence. Now if you'll excuse me, I'd like to finish dinner with my mom. We're having breakfast for dinner. It's our thing." The man smiled and politely turned back to his mother.

Harrison, Caroline, and Padraig absorbed the man's sage-like wisdom for a moment until Stella the server arrived with a frown. "Excuse me," she nagged. "You may not seat yourself. Others are waiting. I'll be happy to add you to the list."

"No," said Caroline. "We were just leaving. Sorry for the trouble."

Stella looked over at the man. "Were these children bothering you, Mr. Seacrest?"

The man waved his hand as if to say it was no trouble.

As Harrison, Caroline, and Padraig got up to go, Harrison stopped at the man's table. Something about what he said didn't sit right, and Harrison wanted clarification. "Sorry to interrupt again," Harrison said. "But I was just thinking...how do you explain when people win the lottery? I mean, that can only be luck, right?"

The man leaned toward Harrison, and Harrison was immediately taken by his wonderful fragrance. He speared a sausage with his fork and pointed it at Harrison. "You don't win the lottery, my friend. The lottery wins *you*."

40

RIVER STREET

Harrison, Caroline, and Padraig poured out of the Waffle House. The sun had set, and the sky was pink in the west. Things started to look familiar to Harrison. By his estimates, they were only a few blocks away from the Italian Cafe where all of their troubles started.

"This way," Harrison said, leading them across Bay Street to River Street.

As they headed toward the hotel, they developed a plan. "The first thing we need to do," Harrison proposed, "is check in with our parents. They're probably wondering where we are, and saying hi should buy us some time."

"Sure. And then all we need is to find some gold. Got any nuggets of gold lying around?" Caroline wondered sarcastically.

Harrison turned quiet in thought. Where did the Chancellor expect a couple of kids to find gold? Gold was expensive. They couldn't exactly walk into a store and use their allowance. Between the two of them, they only had about $40 —and that was the money left over from lunch, which

Harrison planned on giving back to his new Aunt Judy. Did Chancellor Patunia expect them to steal the gold? What good would it do them to break the law and get tossed in jail? Harrison was stuck.

Caroline suddenly thought of something. "I have some gold earrings my mom gave me for my birthday. I can just grab those. I never wear them anyway, so she won't even know they're gone. It's no big deal."

"Are you sure?" Harrison asked, hopeful. Though their luck seemed to have changed, Harrison couldn't believe Caroline would so easily part with a nice birthday gift like that. "You don't have to do that. We can figure out something else."

"Maybe if we had more time. I just want to get this over with as soon as possible. I feel terrible that your brother and George and that Uber driver are locked up like prisoners."

Harrison couldn't argue with her. They should get everyone home as soon as possible, no matter what it took.

As they turned up River Street, crowds of grown-ups walked the sidewalks festively. They wore lots of green and had multicolored beads draped around their necks. Some of them carried long neon plastic water bottles, though it didn't seem like they were filled with water. Vendors grilled sausages and deep fried alligator tails under pop up tents. In the distance somewhere a band cranked out a rock 'n roll version of an Irish folk song.

Padraig took in all of the sites and sounds and smells. "Maybe it wouldn't be so bad to live here. Everyone looks to be having a splendid time. Look at all those colorful beads. The lights and the noise, it is all so very...intoxicating."

Just then, two young women in matching pink wigs, green tuxedos, and sparkly orange boots climbed onto stilts and started walking around two full meters off the ground. Padraig couldn't believe what he was witnessing. "People can be anything they want to be in Waterworld."

"You can be anything you want anywhere you live," Harrison said earnestly. "You're already doing that."

"I am?" Padraig wondered.

"Your house is the most wonderful house in all of Greenland," Caroline agreed. "At least among the houses I've seen. Are there any other houses like yours?"

Padraig considered her question, and could think of no other house similar to his own—at least not in his township, which he rarely traveled away from. His house was very unique, and that made him different. But by being different it was impossible to fit in. So he stopped trying.

"Greenland is a big place, right?" Harrison asked.

Padraig nodded. "It's as big as Waterworld."

"Well then maybe there are other leprechauns like you. Have you ever thought of that?"

Padraig had not, in fact, thought of that. He only knew his own community, and those in his community were very different—with different likes, different tastes, different hobbies, different houses. But maybe there were others somewhere that liked color on their homes and enjoyed the occasional chai latte. Padraig suddenly felt something he had not felt in a long time: *hope*.

41

THE LOBBY BAR

The hotel lobby buzzed with activity. It was Friday night, and excited St. Patrick's Day vacationers milled about as a pianist played old standards on the shiny black grand piano.

Harrison and Caroline peeked through the glass doors. They decided it was probably best for Padraig to wait outside, and Padraig agreed. As Harrison and Caroline headed into the lobby, they were quickly spotted and waived over by Mom and Dale sitting with friends by the lobby bar.

"I'll handle my mom," Harrison whispered to Caroline as they walked over. "She's like the best lie detector in history, so let's try to keep it short and sweet."

Caroline nodded as they entered the lounge area.

"Hi guys. Where is your brother?" Mom asked.

Mom seemed to be in a really good mood. *This should be easy*, Harrison thought as he reminded himself that a lie is not a complete and total lie if it is a little bit true. "He's outside with George," he said. Technically, it wasn't a lie because Max and George were *technically* outside of the hotel. In all truth, they were *technically* outside of this dimension. In any case, Mom's radar-like lie detection skills had been compromised by the stress of her wedding weekend, so it didn't much matter.

"Okay, well, we just saw Grandma and Stanley. They're in the room. Why don't you guys head up and order some chicken fingers or something. You guys be good." Mom smiled and returned to her conversation with Dale and their friends. It was almost as if she was trying to get rid of them.

"Is it okay if we hang out in George's room tonight?" Harrison asked. He didn't want to raise any suspicion, but he also wanted to cover all of his bases. If the mission took longer than expected, he would need a solid alibi.

"Fine," Mom said. "We're going to dinner and won't be back 'til late, so just tell Grandma."

Caroline leaned over to Harrison. "Let's just get my earrings and get out of here."

Harrison nodded in agreement. They were wasting time.

"There you are!" a woman's voice called across the lobby. Harrison and Caroline spun around to see Caroline's mom speed-walking over to them, dressed for a nice dinner.

"Hi Mom," Caroline stated nonchalantly.

"Hi Aunt Judy," Harrison stated all too agreeably.

"*Aunt Judy*, I love it!" Judy yawped, pulling Harrison into a side hug. Maybe it was because it was Friday, or maybe it was because it was the wedding weekend, but for whatever reason grown-ups are always in a great mood in the lobby bar of a hotel.

"May I hang out with Harrison and Max tonight?" Caroline asked politely, looking up at her mother. And then her face turned white and her eyes nearly fell out of her face. Her mother was wearing the earrings—*Caroline's* gold earrings.

"Yes of course," Judy stated, but then she noticed Caroline seemed distraught. "Is everything okay, dear?"

"Um. Yes. Fine. Everything's fine...Are those my earrings?"

Judy turned her head and touched one ear lobe. "Yes! I found them in the bathroom. I haven't seen you wear them, so I figured I'd give them a spin tonight. What do you think? I haven't worn dangly earrings in so long." She took a cleansing deep breath, sending away all of her grown-up stress if only temporarily as Caroline stood idly watching the teardrop-shaped gold swing with her mother's movements. "It's good to get out. I'm feeling relaxed for the first time since I don't know how long." She brandished the gold earrings between her fingertips once more.

"The van is here!" Dale announced.

Mom gave Harrison a kiss on the head. "Say goodnight to your brother for us."

And Judy gave Caroline a kiss on the head. "Don't stay up too late."

The rest of the grown-ups quickly finished their beverages and headed for the valet area. Harrison watched Mom and Judy walk out together, arm-in-arm, and the gold earrings on Judy's ear lobes bounced and dangled tauntingly as the grown-ups disappeared out of the lobby. And just like that, Harrison and Caroline's grand plan to rescue Max, George, and Jack had been foiled.

42

LUCKY ONES

The elevator doors opened, and Harrison and Caroline climbed in and pushed the button for the fifth floor. A tall man with a green top hat, green sunglasses, and a green muscle shirt followed them on and pushed the button for the third floor. Harrison and Caroline stood quietly as the elevator rose.

DING. The elevator doors opened on the third floor and the man stepped off. As he exited, Harrison and Caroline noticed a message written on the back of his shirt: *The more you sweat, the luckier you get.*

Caroline pushed the door-close button. "What are we gonna do?"

Harrison stared up at the numbers above the doors. "Grandma has a gold watch. Stanley gave it to her."

"Do you think if we asked and maybe gave her some explanation, she'd give it to us?"

"Explanation?" Harrison sighed defeatedly. What explanation could they possibly give for needing her very expensive and very favorite gold watch?

DING. The doors opened to the fifth floor.

"What are you going to do?" Caroline asked as they stepped off the elevator.

Harrison did not want to answer that question. He didn't even want to think about it.

"Are you going to steal it?"

"Yeah. Unless you can think of something else." Harrison tried to justify stealing something from his grandmother. "It's just a watch. It's not the end of the world," he said to no one in particular, as if simply putting those words out into the universe might help him believe it.

They moved through the hallway somberly, passing a room where a party seemed to be going on. Music vibrated through the door, and Caroline recognized the Lana Del Rey song, which a friend from her skating team had included in a birthday mix months before. It was the last time Caroline had seen any of her figure skating friends. Her shoulders sagged as she suddenly missed her friends.

"Blame it on me," Caroline insisted. "I've been getting into a lot of trouble lately. I'll say I took it and that I meant to give it back but then lost it. And then I'll offer to pay for it, but your grandmother will likely forgive me because I'm young and my parents just got divorced and I'll probably be grounded for the rest of the year—but it's all my fault that we're in this mess anyway. It's worth it if it means getting Max and George and the Uber guy back safely, right?"

They stopped outside the hotel room door. Harrison couldn't think of anything to say. He was already ashamed of what he was about to do, but he had no other options left. In order to get out of this mess in time for his mother's wedding, he needed to steal his grandmother's favorite gold watch.

43

PRISONERS IN A GOLD CAGE

Chancellor Patunia and Patrica had left the Chancellor's Chambers a short while ago. It had only been about forty-five minutes, but to Max, George, and Jack, it felt like they had been caged in the gold cell for a lifetime. Jack sat cross-legged while Max paced anxiously. George approached the iridescent gold wiring of the cage and dragged her little fingers across it.

"You know, Flappy," she started, gently tugging on the gold threads, "seems like more often than not that when I hang out with you, I end up being someone's prisoner."

Max thought about the time he and George had been locked in Jack's RV. As unnerving as it was back then, it gave Max and George some time to bond. Max remembered it fondly. Since then, they had spent a little bit of time together, whenever George could make it down from the North Pole. But they were usually able to stay out of trouble.

Jack groaned. "What are the chances we never see Earth again?"

"Harrison will think of something." Max had all of the confidence in the world in his brother.

"Well, if he doesn't, then I'm good staying here because if I don't make it back in time for my meeting with the parole officer, then I'll be in some serious doo-doo." Jack started to think about what life would be like as a Greenlander. He would certainly be the tallest. Silver lining, he thought.

Just then, Patricia returned with three leprechaun-sized mugs of tea on a tray and a book. She offered George the tray through one of the wider holes, then sat down on one of the steps that led up to the Chancellor's throne. She held up the book for Max, George, and Jack to see.

"Alice's Adventures In Wonderland." She looked at the book affectionately. "Padraig brought this back from Waterworld for me one time after he lost a pocketful of gold. He thought it would help things with the Chancellor. He still got in trouble, though." She flipped through the first few chapters to a bookmark. "I do love to read," she offered. "Would you like me to read to you?"

44

GRANDMA'S GOLD WATCH

The hotel door swung open, and Grandma greeted Harrison and Caroline with a bright smile. Harrison quickly noted that Grandma was not wearing her watch.

"Hello darlings! Come in, come in," she announced, holding the door open for the kids. "Where's Max-y Boy?"

Harrison continued his true-ish lie that Max was still hanging out with George somewhere. "I just needed to stop by for a quick minute to, uh, change my shirt. Then we're gonna head to George's room."

"Fine by me," Grandma said. "We're about to run down for some dinner. Are you guys hungry?"

"Um, no thanks," Harrison uttered as he and Caroline moved further into the hotel room. He was unable to look his grandmother in the eye.

"We had a big lunch," Caroline explained, half sitting on the bed. She watched as Harrison quietly cased the room.

"Stanley, this is Dale's niece, Caroline."

Stanley looked up from an article he was reading in the

latest issue of Wired Magazine and smiled kindly. "Pleased to meet you. Staying out of trouble, are we?"

Harrison chuckled nervously as he casually scanned the surface of the desk in the corner and the square night table between the beds. The gold watch was on neither. He eyed the little table beside Stanley. Nothing. He checked the top of the dresser. Nothing there, too. He reached into his suitcase and removed a shirt. "I'm gonna change," he said unnecessarily, and he moved into the bathroom.

He switched on the light and threw his clean shirt over his shoulder. On the left side of the sink stood his and Max's electric toothbrushes, toothpaste, and sunscreen. On the right side of the sink stood a small mountain of skin care creams, hair products, makeup, perfume, and toiletries surrounding a few pairs of earrings, a necklace, and...a gold watch.

There it was. Grandma's gold watch. Just lying there like a helpless kitten, minding its own business.

Harrison stared at the watch. It looked new and smooth and shiny. It looked like a gift given out of love. The second hand tick-tick-ticked, and suddenly the only thing Harrison could hear was the tick-tick-ticking of the watch. He didn't want to touch it, but he had to. He couldn't believe he was about to steal something from his one and only grandmother. And he couldn't believe he was going to participate in a plot to blame Caroline for the thievery.

He turned to the mirror and looked at himself as the tick-tick-ticking grew louder and louder. His eyes stung as he stared at himself. Who was this boy in the mirror? What had he become? How did fate deliver him to this moment? Maybe Padraig was right about luck, fortune, and fate, and maybe the nice smelling man at Waffle House was dead wrong. Maybe luck is what powered everything in the world. Maybe some people were destined to be unlucky, and maybe Harrison was destined to be one of those people.

TICK-TICK-TICK. Harrison reached out and grabbed the gold watch. The metal casing seemed to burn in his palm.

TICK-TICK-TICK. He looked at it in his hand and thought about how Grandma would feel after she learned her favorite gold watch, a gift from Stanley, had suddenly gone missing.

TICK-TICK-TICK...TICK-TICK-TICK...TICK-TICK- TICK.

But then, compelled to do the right thing, Harrison placed the watch back on the counter.

45

HANDFASTED

Harrison exited the bathroom. The shirt that he grabbed from his suitcase was still flung over his shoulder. He looked at Caroline and shook his head. He couldn't go through with it. He couldn't take his Grandma's prized gold watch.

Caroline nodded subtly, relieved. Even though they needed gold to bring back to Greenland in exchange for Max, George, and Jack's freedom, she didn't quite like the thought of having to steal it.

Grandma slipped on her shoes as Stanley pulled on a blazer. "We'll be down at the lounge," Grandma announced. "Feel free to come by for a burger." She moved past Harrison and went into the bathroom where she found her gold watch and pulled it on. She checked the time as she returned. "I'm due for more protein."

She came out of the bathroom and tugged on the shirt over Harrison's shoulder. "I thought you were going to change."

Harrison stood there, dejected. He had no plan for getting his brother and George and Jack back from Greenland, which also meant he may be responsible for getting Padraig banished from his home.

Grandma studied Harrison a moment. Being both a grandmother *and* a mom, she knew when her grandson was troubled. "Why so glum?" she asked.

Harrison shrugged, yanking the shirt off his shoulder and throwing it at his suitcase.

"Cheer up! Your mom and Dale are tying the knot in exactly two days. It's a wonderful time!" Grandma kissed Harrison on the head and moved for the door with Stanley.

Harrison finally snapped out of his funereal daze. "What does that mean? 'Tying the knot'? People say it all the time, and I know it means getting married. But what does getting married have to do with knots?"

Grandma's eyebrows raised ever so slightly. "Beats me, son. Stan-baby, got any idea?"

"Well, yes," Stanley stated authoritatively. "There are actually a good number of different explanations, but the one I know comes from the Irish tradition of handfasting."

That was a word Caroline had never heard before. "Handfasting?" she asked curiously.

Stanley explained, "It's an old Celtic custom. It's what folks in Ireland did when they got married. During the ceremony, the man and the woman would hold hands and someone would tie a ribbon or rope around their wrists to symbolize unity. It's what common folks did before the big jewelry corporations got involved and invented wedding rings."

Harrison's eyes lit up like fireworks. He suddenly and unexpectedly had the solution to his big, big problem.

46
RETURN TO CASTLE GREENLAND

H arrison and Caroline raced out of the hotel and ran
down the half-moon driveway to the sidewalk,
which was lined by a neatly manicured row of
bushes. They stopped at a small opening and stepped onto the
grass.

Harrison peered through the shadows, but his eyes hadn't
fully adjusted to the darkness. "*Padraig,*" he whispered
urgently. "*Are you there?*"

"Do you have the gold?" Padraig said, stepping out of the
shadows. His eyes looked hopeful.

Harrison and Caroline smiled and nodded. Padraig
reached into his coat pocket and removed a thin, compact gold
net and swung it around the three of them like a blanket and
—FLOOP—they disappeared.

In an instant, Harrison, Caroline, and Padraig reappeared a
short distance from Jack's Uber car on the outskirts of town.
The sun had set, and the lamps in town glowed yellow-orange.
They raced through the township toward Castle Greenland,
running with great determination.

Ahead, crowds of leprechauns filled into the road from the Tavern. This concerned Padraig very much. Every night for the last week, the Tavern grew more crowded as all of Greenland prepared for St. Patrick's Day. It was the biggest day of celebration in Greenland, after all. Padraig had not attended, but he could hear the celebration all the way from home. He preferred quiet evenings, which gave him time to read gardening books and practice the lute.

Padraig held out his hand to slow their pace. He pulled them to the side of the road where they caught their breath by a lamp post.

"What's going on?" Caroline asked.

"It's a St. Patrick's Day celebration," Padraig explained.

"St. Patrick's Day isn't for two more days," Harrison noted.

"In Greenland, most leprechauns celebrate St. Patrick's Day every night beginning the first of March."

Initially this didn't make sense to Harrison, but the more he thought about it, the more it became less perplexing. It seemed logical that in a land of leprechauns, they would celebrate the one holiday in the calendar year that made the most sense to them. Harrison thought about Christmas and how each year, Dad would start playing Christmas music in the house the day after Thanksgiving. Without realizing it, Harrison pressed his hand against his chest, savoring the memory.

"We should go around," Padraig suggested. "It will take a little longer, but going through that crowd might really slow us down."

Harrison and Caroline knew Padraig didn't want to face the leprechauns for fear of being made fun of again. They felt bad that he was teased earlier in the day. They wanted to tell him to stand up for himself. They wished the other leprechauns could see how interesting Padraig was. He had so many colors to show.

But at this point, the mission was more important than the man. They needed to get to Castle Greenland as soon as possible, and if sneaking around a crowd of rowdy leprechauns meant getting there faster, then Harrison and Caroline were all for it.

So Padraig led Harrison and Caroline off the road and into the wooded area that surrounded the east side of town. They charged down a long path and dodged roots and low hanging branches. Had they not been so determined to get to Castle Greenland, they might have been spooked by the shadowy, misty woods.

They reached the first short hill and charged up. Caroline slipped on the dew, and Harrison lent a hand to stabilize her. Padraig's footing had been solid, which he attributed to Caroline's boots.

"Do you want your boots back?" He asked kindly.

"It's okay," Caroline stated. "I'll be fine—let's go!"

They ran up and down the two other hills to the castle door. They pushed it open and raced into the reception area and through the door to the Council Chambers. They charged across the empty Council Chambers to the Chancellor's door, which was oddly propped open. They sprinted up the stairs and ran into the large throne room where Chancellor Patunia relaxed in her throne while Patricia read "Alice's Adventures In Wonderland."

"Harrison!" Max shouted.

Patricia abruptly stopped reading. Chancellor Patunia sat up straight in her throne.

"Well, that didn't take long." Chancellor Patunia stated.

Harrison zeroed in on his brother. "Are you okay?"

"We're fine," George replied. "We enjoyed some very nice breakfast tea and tried some porter cake, and then Patricia started reading to us. It's been rather enjoyable, actually. Except for the whole being-imprisoned-against-our-will thing."

"Alice is about to play croquet with the queen," Jack relayed. "I kinda want to know what happens next, but I'd also really, really, really like to get out of here."

"Do you have the gold?" Chancellor Patunia asked.

"Yes," Harrison replied.

"And is it of significant value?"

"Definitely," Caroline said.

Chancellor Patunia leaned forward and held out her hand. "Well then, let's have it."

Harrison stepped forward. As he passed the glowing gold cage, he eyed Max sorrowfully, which surprised Max. For Max, it seemed the mission was accomplished. He wondered why Harrison wasn't more enthusiastic.

Harrison reached the bottom step and bowed his head. Then he carefully slipped a silver chain off his neck and over his head. And that's when Max realized why Harrison appeared so somber. For, dangling from the silver chain, was Dad's gold wedding ring.

"A gold ring?" Chancellor Patunia quipped, unimpressed. "Do you mean to suggest that tiny unpolished scrap of metal has more significant value than a sizable gold nugget?"

Harrison wasn't simply suggesting it. The ring was in fact the most valuable item Harrison possessed. "It was my father's wedding ring," he stated. "He passed away a few years ago. He gave me this ring before he died. I don't know what it's worth, but it's worth a whole lot to my brother and me. And to my mom."

He looked at the ring in his palm and imagined it on his dad's left hand. "After Dad died, I didn't think my mom could ever be happy again. And then she met Dale, who's kind of weird, but they're best friends now. They got engaged at Christmas, and they're getting married this weekend. The only reason we ended up here in Greenland is because we were in Savannah for their wedding. I put Dad's ring on a chain because I wanted to wear it during the ceremony so he could be there with us...in spirit...so he could be part of the celebration. He only ever wanted my mom to be happy."

Harrison looked around the room. It was quiet and somber. Caroline got sad thinking about her parents. Patricia and Padraig were crying. So was George and Max. Jack pretended like his eye itched so he could wipe a tear away.

Chancellor Patunia rubbed away the mist out of her eyes and stood. She stepped down to where Harrison was standing and placed her hand on his. "What a most heartfelt story, Harrison. It sounds like you and your brother have been through a lot." And then she did something that no one expected.

She took the ring out of Harrison's hand.

"Don't do this," Padraig pleaded as Chancellor Patunia returned to her throne. "Can't you see how sorry they are?"

"We made a deal," Chancellor Patunia decried. "These Waterworlders kept their end of the bargain." She met Harrison's gaze. "I thank you for your honorableness."

"Maybe we can make a different deal," Padraig suggested urgently. "Instead of taking their gold, we can use these Waterworlders as envoys, like ambassadors, and they can do outreach so the Waterworlders won't want gold so much. I mean, what's worth more than gold? Diamonds? Perfect! They can start a campaign against gold and make Waterworlders think diamonds are better." It was a long shot, but Padraig didn't have any better ideas.

"Actually," George chimed in, "there are a lot of humanitarian campaigns against diamonds right now, so probably not the best solution, but we can workshop the idea and come up with something just as good. Like maybe one of the rare earth metals? Prometheum and holmium are pretty hot right now."

"Nonsense," the Chancellor countered. "There is nothing more precious than gold."

Max scratched his head, bothered by the Chancellor's statement. "Well, I can think of a few things. Like family...and friends."

"Love," Harrison added, "and memories."

"Encouragement and support," Caroline said, thinking about her mom.

"Second chances," Jack sighed.

Padraig smiled at his new friends. "The right to live free as you are. Why, I have come to value that very much."

A warm silence settled over the group as they mused over all the wonderful things they had in their lives. Harrison eyed George, wondering if she had anything to add.

George raised her eyebrows. "Bitcoin?" But nobody seemed to know what that was. "Also love. Definitely love, second chances, memories all that."

"Very well," the Chancellor announced, "but a deal's a deal."

"She's right," Harrison said. "I was prepared to do whatever it took to get everyone home in time for the wedding."

The Chancellor fluttered her hand. "You may go now. Patricia, see to it that Padraig has what he needs to get these Waterworlders home, would you?"

And as Patricia led everyone to the door, Chancellor Patunia returned to her throne, dangling the gold ring in front of her face, admiring her new prize. Harrison and Max looked over their shoulders and took one final glance at their dad's wedding ring.

47

THE CELEBRATION

Patricia saw the group through the reception area to the main entrance of the castle. At the door, she handed Padraig something, which Padraig quickly stuffed into his coat pocket.

Outside they could hear the lively noise from town. The St. Patrick's Day celebration seemed to have grown within the last hour, and thousands of leprechauns were now congregated in the Township. There must have been leprechauns from all over Greenland. By the looks of it, they were having a rollicking good time.

"Now this is what I call a party," George observed. "Can we hang out for like five minutes?"

Harrison turned to Padraig, knowing he likes to avoid the crowds. "Would you rather go around?"

Padraig scanned the crowd. There were clusters of leprechauns he did not recognize. They looked very different than the local leprechauns.

"Padraig, are you seeing this?" Caroline directed Padraig's attention to a clan of leprechauns dressed colorfully from head to toe. They were dancing and singing and jigging with all of the other leprechauns. One of them furiously played the lute. In addition to the typical brown and green attire most leprechauns in Padraig's township wore, these leprechauns incorporated pinks and yellows and blues and reds into their outfits. All of their colors were on display.

Padraig couldn't believe it. He had never experienced this before. But he had always avoided the celebrations for St. Patrick's Day, so how would he know? He moved past the group and headed directly for the celebration. George and Max raced after. Harrison and Caroline both shrugged and started down the hill.

Jack scratched his head curiously. "We're going to the party?" Nobody answered, so Jack followed behind the group. "Can we just all agree to not get into any trouble please?"

They moved over the hillscape into the Township. Padraig was greeted kindly by the new leprechaun faces in the crowd. Caroline could see they admired his Ugg boots and purple overalls. While the humans got a few strange looks, the leprechauns did not show any fear, for they welcomed everyone into their celebration. They pulled the humans into their jig circle and insisted the Waterworlders dance with them. Harrison had never jigged before in his life but as soon as he started he decided that it wouldn't be the last time. Max took to it quite easily, and Caroline spun in the air on one foot like she was on the ice. George high-fived whomever she could, and even Jack caught a dose of boogie fever.

They danced into the night, but then Padraig remembered they had important business ahead. He bowed to his new friends and excused himself with the others. Then they headed down the road toward Jack's car.

48

GOODBYE GREENLAND

Padraig guided Harrison, Max, Caroline, George, and Jack back to Jack's car. The noise of the celebration faded in the distance, and the sky above was black and speckled with white stars. The air was cool on their faces, which were sweaty from dancing.

The silence got Padraig thinking. He still felt badly that Harrison had to give away something he treasured so dearly. "I'm sorry I couldn't be more helpful with Chancellor Patunia," Padraig said.

Harrison nodded his head. "Thanks for trying."

"Did you see how quickly Queenie McGreeny shut down rare earth metals?" George complained. "I'll just say this—the superpowers of the world ain't making lasers and infrared with *gold*."

They arrived at Jack's car, and Padraig removed the Uggs from his feet. He handed them to Caroline. "Here," he said sorrowfully. "It's the very least I can do for getting all of you into this mess."

Caroline held the boots in her hand and rubbed her

thumb across the soft suede leather. She thought about how many compliments Padraig received from the other leprechauns. She thought that maybe the boots could be just the icebreaker Padraig needed to strike up a conversation with a new potential friend.

"You should keep them," she said, handing the boots back to Padraig. "If it gets you noticed for being a really cool leprechaun around here, then I'm all for it. Besides, you reminded me that I don't have to be afraid to be myself...that I shouldn't be afraid to show all the colors of my rainbow, right?"

Padraig smiled wide, delighted by his gift. He pulled the boots onto his feet, did a short little jig, and then he wrapped his arms around Caroline's legs and squeezed her into a hug. Caroline grinned. She hadn't been hugged by a friend like that since she placed second in the individual short program in the County Figure Skating Competition. She missed the feeling she got when skating her best, and in that moment, she promised herself she would get back on the ice as soon as she could.

They each said their goodbyes to Padraig and individually thanked him for his assistance. Then they piled into Jack's car. He started the car as Padraig watched from the side of the road. Inside the car, everyone waved. Harrison saw Padraig reach into his coat pocket and remove something that looked like a garage opener. He pointed the device at the car, pressed, and—FLOOP!

In the blink of an eye, the car reappeared in the corner of an empty bank parking lot. A white light from the bank's sign illuminated the area. The clock on the car stereo read 9:39 PM.

Harrison, Max, and Caroline looked around, hoping for a landmark they might recognize. It was nighttime, and it was quiet. They must not have reappeared in Savannah, Harrison wondered, because they would've certainly heard all of the sounds of the St. Patrick's Day weekend celebrations. Jack checked his navigation system. George checked her texts.

"Got a couple texts from Jenny and Dale," George reported. "No sign of panic. I'd call this lukewarm concern." She looked at Harrison and Caroline. "Nice job covering, guys."

"We're in Richmond Hill!" Jack shouted. "That's like thirty minutes from Savannah. I'll take that over Augusta any day."

By all measures, Harrison, Max, Caroline, and George would be back well before anyone would get worried. And Jack wouldn't have any problems meeting with his parole officer come Monday.

They each took a deep, cleansing breath. *They did it.* Somehow they did it. Whether it was due to good luck, fate, fortune, or chance—somehow, some way, they made back from an entirely different dimension. Everything was going to be okay. Jack fired up the car, turned around to his passengers to confirm they were wearing their seatbelts, and started for Savannah.

49

FIVE STARS

Savannah was abuzz with activity for the St. Patrick's Day weekend, and some of the roads were closed. The drive took a little longer than expected because of the crowds in the street. Jack turned into the busy valet area of the Savannah Country Inn, and Harrison, Max, Caroline, and George unbuckled their seatbelts.

"Thanks for the ride, stretch," George announced. "Five stars, all the way."

"I sincerely appreciate that," Jack said. "But I hope I never have to give you people a ride ever again." He smiled warmly.

Harrison patted Jack on the shoulder. "Good luck with everything, Jack. You're a really great guy."

Jack chuckled nervously. "I'd love to congratulate your mom and Dale, but I'd rather they never knew I existed. Have a great weekend everybody." Suddenly his Uber driver app lit up with a request for a ride. "Whoa. It's gonna be a good night." And just like that, Jack's luck had turned. He took one last look at the gang and waved warmly. Then he shifted the car into drive and motored away.

Harrison thought about how crazy it was that they ran into Jack so randomly in Savannah and how lucky they were to have him as their driver. He couldn't help thinking that would be the last time he got to hang out with Jack and got a little sad at the notion of never seeing him again. But no matter what the future held, Harrison hoped for nothing but the best for Jack.

As Jack drove away, a large van pulled into the valet area, and Mom, Dale, Judy, and their friends climbed out, spirits high. *Wow*, Harrison thought. *What luck.*

50

MARCH 16, 2014

I t was about an hour before the wedding ceremony had been scheduled to start, and Harrison and Max entered the back of the church. They wore their new navy blue suits and tugged on their striped red ties that matched Dale's.

Harrison remembered the last time he and Max had to wear a suit. It was Dad's funeral. At least this time was a much happier occasion, Harrison thought. He still felt badly that he had to give away his father's wedding ring. It would have been nice to have that for the ceremony, but Harrison also knew that Dad was there in spirit no matter what.

Judy arrived with Caroline. They were both wearing tasteful Spring dresses and their hair looked fancy. Harrison thought it was strange to see Caroline in a dress, and Caroline thought it was strange to see Harrison and Max in suits. Weddings were weird like that.

"You two look very handsome," Judy complimented. "I'm just going to check and see if your mom needs anything."

Judy disappeared into the anteroom where Mom had been putting the finishing touches on her hair and makeup. At the front of the church, the door opened and in walked George in a forest green, crushed velvet tuxedo. Had that same tuxedo been on a regular sized adult, it would have looked ridiculous. But somehow, George pulled it off.

"Cool tuxedo," Max said as George approached.

"Thanks, flappy. I figured I could knock out two birds with one stone this weekend with one suit. Tomorrow is gonna be off the chain on River Street."

"Looking good, everyone!" Grandma called from across the church as she arrived with Stanley. They took their seats in the first pew in front of the altar.

"Boys!" Mom called from the anteroom, and then she appeared in the doorway in her shimmering white wedding dress. It wasn't too poofy or too satiny or too flowing or too long. It was just right for the occasion. She was absolutely glowing, and Harrison couldn't remember the last time she looked so happy.

She stepped out and air-kissed her sons so her makeup didn't get smudged. And then she air-kissed Caroline and George.

"You look beautiful, Aunt Jenny," Caroline said gracefully.

Mom's heart melted slightly at the sound of her new title, *Aunt Jenny*. Then she turned to Harrison. "I was telling your Aunt Judy about you bringing your father's wedding ring."

Aunt Judy smiled warmly. "What a thoughtful idea, Harrison."

"May I see it?" Mom asked.

Harrison froze. What was he going to do? He didn't have the ring. It was in Greenland, an entirely separate dimension. He wanted to come clean to his mom, but what could he possibly say? If he told her the truth—that he didn't have his dad's ring because he had to hawk it to the Chancellor of

Greenville so he could bail his brother and George and Jack out of leprechaun jail—she'd assume he was lying, and she'd be very disappointed that he lied to her on her wedding day. Harrison absolutely did not want to disappoint his mother on her wedding day.

Luckily, Mom got called back to the anteroom by the hairstylist. And that's when something caught Harrison's attention. It was a flash of light, like someone was angling a sunbeam off of a mirror directly in his face. He wasn't sure what it was at first, but then Caroline saw it, too. Was someone trying to get their attention? They moved to the side door of the church, and Max and George followed.

Outside, they looked around. A squirrel pranced across a tree branch. Some leaves gently rolled about the grass in the Savannah breeze. The flash of light shined in their eyes again from the parking lot, and something disappeared around the corner. They hustled over and turned down the alley. It was a dead end. No sign of life—just some crates stacked against the brick wall next to a half-full dumpster.

They moved closer. George covered her nose, repulsed by the smell. Caroline and Max did, too.

And that's when Harrison spotted it.

There, on the corner of the dumpster, dangled a silver chain linked around a gold wedding ring.

Dad's wedding ring.

51

A SHINE IN THE MULCH

M ax, Caroline, and George headed back into the church. Harrison paused in order to wipe some dust off the ring with the smooth fabric on the inside of his jacket. He wanted to ensure the ring looked its best for Mom. He stood there, admiring the ring and thinking about his dad. After a moment, he lifted the chain over his head and slipped the chain around his neck. He tucked the ring into the narrow space between his collar and his skin, then started for the church.

But then something else caught his attention.

Just under the bushes in the wet brown mulch sat a small shiny object no larger than a golf ball. Harrison crouched down to get a better look. He squinted as the object reflected the sun into his eye, and then he shifted to dodge the reflection. And that's when he saw it. There, alone on the ground, sat a small nugget of gold. Harrison leaned over and extended his hand—

And then he thought better of it.

He stood up, keeping his eyes on the gold. He looked

around. *What did Padraig get himself into this time?* he wondered.

He scooped a small mound of mulch next to the gold, hoping to conceal it just enough so that no human would find it. Hopefully, if it was Padraig that lost this gold—and Harrison had no reason to believe it could have been any other leprechaun—then he'd soon be back to claim it before any human picked it up.

Harrison wiped the remnants of the mulch off his glossy leather shoe and turned for the church. Inside, he could hear Mom calling for him. As he stepped into the side door, he saw Mom standing with Dale and Max and George and Grandma and Stanley and Aunt Judy and Caroline. He pulled the ring out from under his shirt and dangled it so Mom could see, then he tucked it back in and smiled. Right then and there in that moment, Harrison felt like the luckiest kid alive.

MARCH 17, 2015

"Harrison! Max! Dinner's ready!"

Harrison and Max raced downstairs. The hearty aroma of Dale's famous shepherd's pie had permeated through the house for the last hour, and Harrison and Max couldn't wait to dig in. As they arrived in the dining room, they noticed Mom and Dale were already seated.

"I hope you guys are hungry," Dale said, scooping portions onto plates.

"I could eat a horse," Mom said eagerly.

"Gross!" Max laughed.

Harrison took his plate from Dale and set it down on a green satin placemat that Mom brought out special for St. Patrick's Day. As Harrison blew the steam away from his dinner, he noticed Mom and Dale were holding hands. Yesterday was their first wedding anniversary, and Harrison couldn't believe it had already been a year since his and Max's adventures in Greenland.

"Boys," Mom stated, starting into her shepherd's pie. "You know how we were planning to visit Dale's family in Georgia this fall? Well, we think it might be better if we moved up the trip to June."

Max shrugs his shoulders as he chewed a mouthful of food. "Okay."

"But I thought you said we were gonna go in the fall because it's really pretty down there that time of year," Harrison said.

"Well, yeah, it is," Dale stated, squeezing Mom's hand, "but it's pretty in the summer, too."

Mom set down her fork and lifted her shamrock-patterned napkin to wipe her mouth. "We also wanted to make sure we get the chance to see everyone before the baby comes."

Harrison and Max stared at their mom. Max was confused. Harrison furrowed his brow, piecing together the information. It seemed like there was a detail or two missing. But then his brain filled the gap and concluded with all certainty that HIS MOM WAS PREGNANT.

Harrison's eyes just about popped out of his head.

Max finally blinked and turned to Dale to confirm: "Mom's gonna have a baby?"

"You guys are the first to know," Dale said proudly.

Harrison knew his life was about to change. He didn't know how and he didn't know when, but everything he knew about babies drew him to the conclusion that it would be sometime in the next year. He offered a sincere congratulations.

Mom smiled happily and eyed Dale. "And get this—she's due on Halloween."

"*She*?" Max asked.

"*Halloween*?" Harrison wondered.

And though Harrison didn't know for sure, he suspected Halloween this year may be one he'll never forget.

Thanks for joining Harrison, Max, George, and Caroline on their adventures! Did you enjoy LUCKY DAY? Here's what you can do next... If you loved the book and have a moment to spare, I would really appreciate a short review. Your help in spreading the word is gratefully received!

If you enjoyed LUCKY DAY, be sure to check out NAUGHTY WEEK, the first book in the "Naughty Week" series. It can be found at your local library or wherever books are sold.

For news and updates about upcoming projects, sign up at mattdonnellywrites.com

Made in the USA
Coppell, TX
01 March 2022